19 Short Stories by Stephen Geez

Comes this Time to Float

19 Short Stories by Stephen Geez

Stephen Geez

Fresh Ink Group
Guntersville

Comes This Time
To Float

Fresh Ink Group
An Imprint of:
The Fresh Ink Group, LLC
1021 Blount Avenue #931
Guntersville, AL 35976
Email: info@FreshInkGroup.com
FreshInkGroup.com

Edition 1.0   2019

Cover and book design by Stephen Geez / FIG
Layout by Amit Dey
Cover art by Anik / FIG
Associate publisher Lauren A. Smith / FIG

Cataloging-in-Publication Recommendations:

FIC029000 **FICTION** / Short Stories (single author)
FIC019000 **FICTION** / Literary
FIC066000 **FICTION** / Small Town & Rural

Library of Congress Control Number: 2020931487

ISBN-13: 978-1-947867-80-2 Softcover
ISBN-13: 978-1-947867-81-9 Hardcover
ISBN-13: 978-1-947867-85-7 Audiobook
ISBN-13: 978-1-947867-82-6 Ebooks

This one is for Dad,
who never stops giving,
and to whom I owe more
than even a writer can put into words.

Acknowledging My Cohorts

It is with humble gratitude that I thank these people for helping me with these stories and with putting together this collection:

Ann E. Stewart, the late managing director of publisher Fresh Ink Group (FIG): Nearly all of these stories were prepped, formatted, submitted, managed, and more by Ann at various times of our long history together. She is remembered fondly by all who knew her. Her influence on how we do things at FIG is timeless.

Beem Weeks, associate publisher, editor, media producer, social-media manager, and more: Beem is the only person I trust to review my material. He offered wondrous feedback for many of these stories. We worked together on choosing, assembling, and tweaking this collection, as well as on producing its promo videos.

Lauren A. Smith, associate publisher, managing director: Lauren keeps Fresh Ink Group humming, even as she works on book projects and more.

Scott Watson, Dizzy, Snake Wagner, Benjamin Wagner, Storyblocks, UnSplash, and more, photographers, artists, pic-shapers—these people and collections added poignant imagery to my prose and to the book's videos.

Stephanie Collins, Traci Sanders, Sooz Burke, Helen Borel, Gordon Bickerstaff, Joseph Ajlouny, Robin Chambers, Vashti Quiroz-Vega, Kent Casey, et alia, hard-core supporters who believe in my work and aren't bashful about spreading the word.

Contents Hereabouts

Sidekick

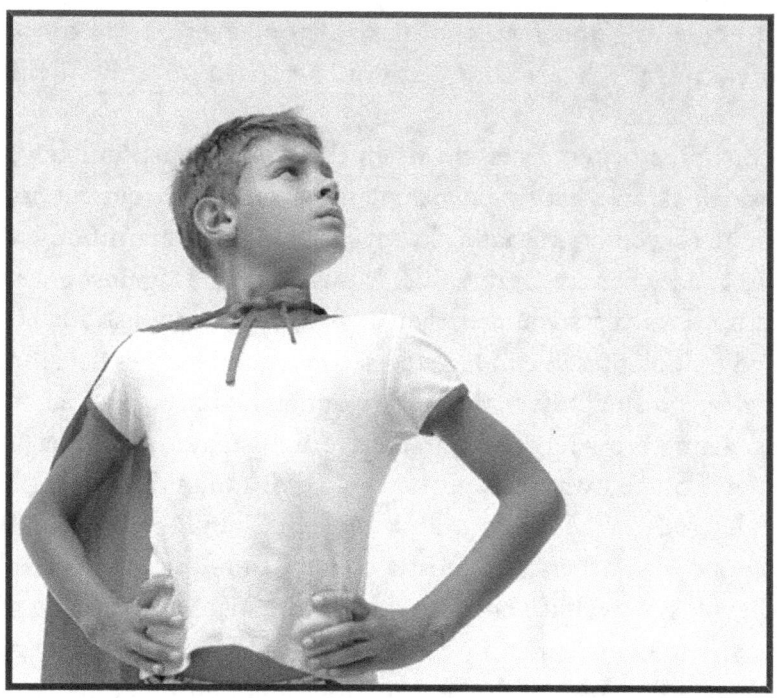

*I wrote this when a favorite literary journal asked me for a short.
It has appeared in several places since. Oh, what differences we
can make in the lives of others—and ourselves, as well.*

$\mathcal{I}$ just figured out something all superheroes should know about our sidekicks.

I happened upon my own sidekick long before I grew up and stepped into the role of hero, way back when I was just a regular suburban kid with no inkling of my destiny as the savior of countless lives. Never a fan of those other heroes who star in their own comic books, I had no idea what a sidekick is supposed to do, let alone how much I would even need one.

And now, after decades working with my own sidekick for the common good, something has gone horribly wrong, and the blood is coming too fast, the injuries too severe, time too short. It's breaking my heart that our era as superhero and sidekick is about to end.

I was nine or ten years old when the world's most unlikely wannabe sidekick and his single-parent mom moved to our town. They set up housekeeping in that leaky rat's nest of an old farmhouse down the dirt road where overgrown fields pushed feebly against encroaching scrub. Two years younger than I, skinny and smallish for his age, he tried to look passable in tattered second-hand clothes usually sized too big or too small. Ever the bully magnet, he liked to pedal around on his chain-throwing rattletrap bicycle, a mismatch of old parts he'd scavenged. Since I was the only boy who didn't taunt him or push him down, he got to where he'd follow me about, hoping to join in while I hung out with others, but mostly content to hover at the periphery. He knew his place, but never acted resentful, instead appearing grateful for the tolerated proximity. No matter how much I ignored him, though, he often seemed to be watching me intently, studying me, as if appraising something only he could see.

Catching me alone with nowhere particular to go one day, he said he had a secret to tell me. He looked around as if worried someone might approach with bad intent. "Not here," he whispered.

Now, as piqued as preteen boys are about mysteries, they're just as skeptical of other boys' promises of intrigue, except that he looked so serious my curiosity won out. "Just tell me," I insisted, but he wiped his nose on his sleeve, then simply looked me straight in the eyes and waited, for once not looking so jumpy and scared.

So for privacy we rode our bikes out to his place where we found his mom outside, standing beside the house, staring blankly at a jumble of rotting planks, apparently perplexed about the scrap-pile's dilemma. Her hair a dirty tangle, clothes on backwards or inside out, she appeared to be lost, or maybe drunk or even insane.

Embarrassed, he dropped his bicycle and urged me to stay back, then approached her cautiously, maybe afraid of spooking her. He took her by the arm, whispered assurances, and led her up to the partly collapsed porch. As if finally recognizing her surroundings, she pushed the door open slowly, focused on him a moment, then drifted inside. I watched through a window as he eased her into a chair, then brought her a glass of water, her hands trembling as she drank. He waited until she settled back and closed her eyes. Where does the picked-on boy retreat for his own reassurance when he's the one caring for his grown-up?

He led me to the big shed beyond the house. He'd cleaned it up, arranged some stick furniture, added several stacks of faded superhero comic books, and achieved a rather clubhouse-like atmosphere. He offered me some crackers from a box and poured cups of Kool-aid from a jug, ice cubes from a cooler under the table. We kicked back, at which time I proceeded to ask any normal ten-year-old's next question.

His cheeks flushed. Tugging at his loose shoelace until it broke, he finally admitted, "She's all right if she takes her medicine, but she can't get 'em when no doctors show up at the clinic. Not taking 'em reg'lar makes the in-betweens worse than never taking 'em at all."

That proved a problem I couldn't solve, so I switched to the main subject. "That's not the secret, is it?"

He shook his head, then stopped fidgeting long enough to look me straight in the eyes again, pausing as if weighing how much he really trusted me. He took a deep breath, lowered his voice, and said, "I got a superpower."

Oh, geez. I eyed the comic books and snorted my disapproval, then decided I might as well have some fun with this. "So? I got superpowers, too."

His eyes widened, and he offered the hint of a grin. "Oh, good. You already know."

"Yeah, I know *everything* in the universe."

His shoulders slumped. "Oh, making fun of me."

I put my hands up. "Sorry. Okay, but you gotta explain first."

He wrinkled his nose and rubbed his forehead, then looked me right in the eyes for a third time. "You can make fun of me, but it won't change the truth. I can see—well, my power is I can see *other* people's powers."

"*Every*body has some?"

"Well, just *you* so far. In everybody else I can see what they *don't* have."

"Just me, huh?"

"Yep," he confirmed, getting up to gaze out the window toward his house. He turned and stood in front of me. "You're going to be a superhero someday, and I'm going to be your sidekick."

I started out amused, then for some odd reason annoyed. "Don't tell anybody that," I warned. I mean, I didn't care if he was crazy as his mom; I just didn't need anybody thinking I was, too.

After that day, I mostly avoided him, though he still persisted at the periphery, practically wearing a *Victimize me!* sign. I even acted mean toward him a few times, just to go along with the crowd, but it always left me feeling bad. It gets kinda hard to show your worst to someone who keeps insisting he sees good in you.

Every time he found a chance at brief privacy, he reminded me he'd be my sidekick whenever I was ready. I didn't get why this mattered so much to him, this skinny little pest who always seemed just a bit "off."

Then one day Todd talked me into riding our bikes out to the kid's place to mess with him a bit, nothing too bad. We found him in his clubhouse, the place vandalized. He was sitting on the floor in the corner, knees up, hugging his legs, rocking, and . . . crying. He looked up, revealing a bloody nose and brow, face scuffed. Todd wanted no part of getting blamed for beating him up, so he immediately took off while I stayed and helped the kid clean himself up, ice from his cooler on the swollen eye, Band-aids over a cut on his arm.

Then I went on a hunt for the offending Roux brothers, and despite improbable odds tilted only by my rage and determination, I left them also in need of ice and Band-aids, both powerfully motivated to avoid further reprisals for messing with *my* sidekick.

He thinks I saved him that day, and though I did make his life a lot better in how he got treated by others, in truth I'm the one who's life changed the most. See, without even starting to believe in the absurd notion of "superpowers," I did get hooked on the idea of stepping up when someone needed my help.

And look how many lives I've saved in the years since, and how many more I've improved because my sidekick never relented in reminding me to pursue my better self.

I took a lot of heat during my teen years for letting him tag along so much, but he never really seemed to have any other friends. Then when his mom got so bad there for a while, *somebody* had to make sure he got enough to eat and had a warm place to crash, especially while lowlifes were taking all-night advantage of her in that leaky rat's nest of an old farmhouse.

Even superheroes have a regular life, a public persona, the need to walk among others without attracting too much attention; so I registered for a dorm room when I started college some hundred miles away. My sidekick followed, despite being under legal age, living here and there, working odd jobs, a child of opportunity and necessity. When I took an apartment second year, he stayed mostly at my place, a tremendous help around the house so I could concentrate on my studies. He spent most of his spare time making a fairly good living, cooking and cleaning and running errands and laundering and servicing cars for some of the more well-to-do students. He always put me first, though.

Not that I asked him to.

No, I never asked, and I did try not to take advantage of him. Those times I maybe sorta did, he seemed not only to understand, but to appreciate the opportunity. Seems that when someone is also working hard to help you achieve your goals, *your* accomplishments become *his*, too; and if you try to make him stop, it hurts you both.

He followed me across the country when I started med school. He proved so successful at his enterprise, he managed to help me and still earn enough from others to score a good place to live and cover his simple tastes. He even temporarily helped me out with a short-term loan once or twice—or maybe three times.

Now, during the year or so Donna lived with me, *she* kept trying to take advantage of his good nature. I resented this because she didn't *need* the help, her chief pursuits being to coast through a couple of easy undergrad classes, spend her daddy's money on clothes, and spin fantasies about being married to a rich doctor someday—my alternate future that didn't hew to the superhero plan. I did come close to telling her the truth a few times, how I secretly nurtured superpowers so my sidekick and I could save the world someday—or at least a small corner of it. The problem solved itself, though, when she found a bauble-coveting second-year resident who liked to spin himself a role in her fantasies of opulent living and enviable social standing.

What's ironic is that I did wind up spending a few years in private practice earning *a lot* of money, but not to spend the way she would have wanted. Then my sidekick and I moved back across the country to a bad neighborhood close to where we grew up. We opened a free clinic in the worst part of town. It's been quite successful, me working day and night, saving and improving lives, my sidekick doing everything else and then some. He's proven near genius at hustling grants and donations, cajoling practitioners at all levels to volunteer their time, and negotiating discounts from providers. In this community, I've become the superhero, and though I'm not sure this is exactly the future that skinny little pest saw, I do think he's satisfied it was worth believing in me. I do know I wouldn't be who I am without him.

Through it all, though, I've had one regret, and now I have two.

The first: My success came too late for his mom. He sat in the corner and cried that day, and no amount of ice or Band-aids or my threatening of bullies could help. If anything good could come from that, maybe it's that it infused him—infused us—with greater determination not to let that happen to others, especially the moms and dads of scared children who have to take charge when they should be the ones cared for.

My second regret: I wasn't prepared for what just happened here tonight, and now the greatest ever superhero/sidekick partnership is about to end.

And now I finally see the truth: I might call him "sidekick," but this good-hearted young man has never been anything but simply my friend.

That picked-on skinny little pest knew he wanted to grow up and help others, but he couldn't do it by himself, so he found one guy with the power to make it happen, the one guy who might not know it yet, but who—with a bit of help and lots of reminding—would grow into the kind of man who accepts and eventually embraces that role. The rare occasions he brought up that whole notion of becoming my sidekick, he always seemed matter-of-fact about it, never any doubt, proud that he would be the one.

And it's breaking my heart to see it end like this.

He stayed late, intending to sleep here in the clinic tonight because we've had break-ins and drug thefts. I came back with some late-night carry-out dinner to find him held at gunpoint, an instant of commotion, shouting, shots fired, and blood, too much blood, worse than a mere clinic can handle, time too short.

Thieves just grabbed the drugs and ran.

And the truth in having the power to save lives means that you also know its limits. You know when a fully equipped trauma center is too far to reach in time, the blood coming too fast.

And he's kneeling over me, and for the third time in all our years I see him crying, but I'm barely holding on, one hand inside myself, trying to stanch the flow to buy some minutes before I bleed out, the other hand clutching his arm, desperate to make him listen.

But he won't, jerking free, calling 911, grabbing a tray of instruments. He's seen me do this. He's been my sidekick.

"My life insur—insurance," I tell him, trying not to choke on the blood. Man, this hurts. "You'll always—always have—money."

Liquid fire, and he cuts into me, turning me to drain the fluid, searching for bleeders, clamping, trying desperately to save me.

"Keep it—keep going—clinic. *Make* others help—you can—"

Dizzy now. Tingling. Sirens in the distance.

He's pushing fluids, trying to keep me from crashing.

"If you have to—" I insist, floating now. "You can—can do it—without me."

They're outside now. Maybe, maybe there *is* a chance. Still, I have to tell him, just in case. He's got my head up, cradling it, whispering assurances.

I try to reach for him, but my arm is numb, somewhere else.

He looks me straight in the eyes, like he always has, and I can't say it yet because he's telling me something. What's he telling me?

What?

"I have one power," he's saying, and he believes it with all his heart. "I can look inside people and see *their* powers. And what I've seen all along, we still got bigger things to do than this clinic."

The police are inside now, all clear for the EMTs to enter.

I'm fading into waves of tingles, but now I wonder if just maybe I'll be able to find my way.

"We got him," one voice says, lifting me.

"*You* did all this?"

Cool air, flashing lights.

"Yeah, he got *all* the bleeders."

Moving fast, siren.

"GSW to the chest!"

People helping others.

"Wow, Doc, you got lucky."

Yeah, back when I was just a regular suburban kid of nine or ten, I got lucky. I can see him out there now, craning to watch, worried but confident.

The one I depend on . . .

Yes, there's something all superheroes should know:

Sidekicks are heroes, too.

Veneer

Okay, I wrote this one for a literary journal, too. They asked for something that addresses class and race. I limited the point of view to one old lady, and I let the narrative reflect her ways of seeing and speaking. I did grow up in the melting-pot of Detroit suburbs in the 1960s, an era when rioting and racial disharmony affected our relationship with the city. The few run-on sentences are on purpose. At times, I've found that adage about the veneer of civilization to be quite the case.

In the end, bad weather turned out to be what pierced the veneer.

Two uniforms pounded on the door, demanding entry and using her name like they had a right. She remained frozen, barely breathing, her stroke-addled leg throbbing, finger twitching on the trigger of Daddy's rifle.

Bam bam bam! "Mizzus Heidway!" came the door-muffled call of Sheriff Dander, his voice a rumble under that drone of wicked downpour shotgunning the tin roof. "Now, y'alls *got* to come with us! They's evacuatin' the whole valley!"

Twenty years since Mama died and left her the house, twenty years since Iris came back to live the South Alabama life she'd fled hoping never to return, twenty years running all her errands in nearby towns to avoid in-yer-business local busybodies, yet now these uniforms had the gall to come uninvited right onto an old woman's property.

"If you're in there, you's *got* to come out now!"

Nothing is what she ever *got* to do, especially for two bullies with badges. She'd seen Sheriff Dander on the news a few times, always under investigation for some kind of brutality. Seems like the kind of person who *wants* to be a cop is the one who has no business being one.

Letting her screen door slam, the intruders retreated into a frenzy of rain. Iris Heidway hobbled to the window and peeked through the curtains. A county van packed with busybodies turned around, then rocked and swayed its way back up the hill, splashing through a frantic gravel-washer streaming down the rutted road. She couldn't see herself climbing in with that mob, or wedged between all those so-and-so's at some makeshift shelter, everybody grabbing and hugging, you'll be okay honey this'll be over soon anything you need just let us know . . . Touchers pretend they're doing something for you, but they're the ones tricked by a fool's notion of connection. Anybody lays a hand on Iris Heidway, he'll be lucky to get it back.

Once the taillights disappeared into swirls of dense downpour, she checked the TV again, same panicky story, storm of the century, worse coming when the hurricane lands tonight, several old dams and earthen-berm reservoirs threatening to fail. Iris Heidway intended to ride this out just fine, thank you very much. *Somebody* needs to protect what's hers.

Looting would break out when the waters receded, especially down these out-of-the-way country roads, unattended homes. Convinced they can get away with it, people will do anything. Scare them, and they'll turn on each other. Thrust them into adversity, hungry and cold and homeless, they'll go savage, predatory, murderous. It's true what they say:

The veneer of civilization is very thin.

Rifle in hand, she limped out to the covered back porch. It did look bad. Normally a tortuous climb several hundred yards downhill to its bank, the river had risen even with the overlook where Granddaddy built this old two-storey tin-roofer some hundred years ago. Muddy water lapped at the back wall of the windowless smokehouse, now converted to her garage.

She sat in the chain-swing and watched a debris-bobbing rager rushing down the main channel beyond the old tree-line. Backwash spun off eddies rolling into her yard and nudging the footings of her house. The rain refused to slack off, even as sky-patches of green and gray dimmed to the purple bruise of dusk. That river never had the gumption to rise even half this much. Worse, it seemed to be having too much fun to stop now.

Surprisingly scared, she headed back inside, but still didn't feel any safer. Surely there wouldn't be enough current to pull down the house if floodwaters backed into this holler. Need be, she could retreat to the second floor, even the attic room with that small dormer window overlooking the slope of corrugated tin.

The power flickered a few times and went out. She worked the panel loose to fetch her only kerosene lamp from that hidey-hole behind the pantry. Stick-matches cluttering a knick-knack tray on the middle-bedroom dresser proved sufficient to light the wick. Relieved to find its eight-hour reservoir full, she regretted never buying that intended can of refill.

A series of bangs, several loud cracks, and a walloping *thump* hurried her from window to window. The fading glow of dusk silhouetted swaying trees and flailing branches. A portion of hillside across the clearing had collapsed like puddin' cake into the roadway. She stepped outside, fouled her shoes in mud the uniforms had tracked onto her covered porch, got sprayed by gusting rain, and retreated to the doorway. Everywhere, sky reflected off the ground . . . water.

From the converted garage, another *thump!* Out the kitchen window she saw him, a figure moving around the roll-up door, pounding the padlocked hasp with something—a rock, maybe—now pushing the door open—

Looters!

One emerged and splashed his way toward the house. Iris grabbed Daddy's rifle and hobbled to the hidey-hole, then closed herself in and slid to the floor. Trying to catch her breath, she aimed the barrel and wished she'd brought the lamp.

Must be quiet.

Wait . . .

They could take whatever they wanted. Meaning, expecting, *intending* to defend her property, now at the critical moment she just wanted to be left alone. *Things is just things*, she decided, blinking through the blur of tears, *but 72 is way too young to die*. Nobody would remember Harold, killed forty-odd years ago. Nobody would remember Cynthia, their baby girl, a wonderful young woman who never saw twenty-five.

In the house now . . .

"Mizzus Heidway!" came the muffled voice, hoping she'd gone. "Mizzus Heidway!"

Room to room, then up the stairs, moving faster now—

Extra words, can't make 'em out.

Sounds in the kitchen, fifteen, ten feet away. "Mizzus Heidway! I know you's here! The lamp in the bedroom's full up, just been lit!" An occupied house wouldn't stop him from robbing the place, doing an old lady harm.

She stifled a sob, stared into blackness, decided she'd not been ready for this after all. The footworn Linoleum floor squeaked.

Closer now.

Her muddy footprints had led him right to her. Too late, her fatal mistake settled about her shoulders, weighing her down.

Scraping on the wall, gentle raps, hollow echoes, silence . . . and the hidey-hole door slid open, white eyes against a dark face, the blinding glare of kerosene flame moving into the opening, her rifle barrel fixed on his forehead.

Eyes wide now, his free hand up, he backed away. "Mizzus Heidway, it's *me*."

"I know who y'are," she said, recalling the gangly teen, seventeen, eighteen maybe. Struggling to her feet, she held the barrel steady, her composure fueled by rage over unrighted wrongs. "You're Caroline's boy, but you ain't about to get away with stealin' from *me* again."

"Whatchoo mean *again?*"

"You know why I fired you and yer grandmaw."

"First off," he said, feigning indignance, "Mamaw's the one worked for you, not me. Ten years, she worked hard, lookin' out since you done had that stroke, and not for much money, neither. All I did was help out sometimes 'cause I *wanted* to."

Iris Heidway knew better. Anybody offers to help for nothing, count on him to come back expecting *some*thing later. Same with people trying to *give* to you: Man with a crust of bread won't offer half unless he figures next time you'll feel guilty about eating a whole slice in front of him. "Help *yourself*, you mean." She brandished the rifle, backing him and the lamp through the dining room and into the front parlor.

"I never took nothin' from you," he argued, setting the lamp on the table. "You broke Mamaw's heart, and never give her no reason why."

"Either you or her, maybe the both of you, took my granddaddy's collection."

"That old box of coins you was allus hidin' here and there?"

"Many of them coins went back to the Civil War. Shop over to Birmin'ham offered me thirteen-thousand dollars, meaning really worth three times that, at least."

"If we stole 'em, then why did me and Mamaw keep livin' in that shack upriver? Why didn't we just light on out of here?"

Water squirted around the front door jamb, rivulets snaking across the hardwood floor. More sloshed from the back door into the kitchen. Rain continued shotgunning that corrugated-tin roof. The lamp's flame guttered.

"You need to go," she said, trying not to panic. "Ain't no call for you to be here."

He shook his head, then turned to gaze out the window. "Was planning to say you's going with me, but now it's too late."

"You can wade. Wade back up to your place."

Genuine surprise creased his features. "That's all washed down the river now."

"What about your grandmaw?"

He moved to another window, pulled back the curtain, and gazed out; then turned to face her, a deep sadness rising in his eyes. "Stroke. Lived two months, been gone a couple weeks now." Louder, he added, "Didn't see you come up to help her like she did you after yours."

Stung, Iris backed up, sat in the overstuffed high-back. "I didn't know," she said quietly.

"She didn't want you to know—didn't want you to see her like that."

"But—but I was her—" She lowered her eyes and watched muddy water creep across the floor, wishing for some way to wash away regret. Finally, she took a deep breath, raised the barrel again, and said, "You can still head up for the road, get a ride."

He shook his head. "Upriver, the bridge is washed out. Downriver, the road'll be under water by now, too dangerous to wade."

"So you *did* have time to go," she accused, standing again, "but you figured I left in the sheriff van, so might as well come loot my house first."

He snorted. "No way you was leavin' in that van, *that* I *know*."

"So you broke into my garage to see if I drove out on my own."

He crossed the room, stopped before her, then carefully reached out and pushed the barrel down toward the floor. "That part you got right," he said, heading back toward the window, sloshing through the spreading pool formed by front-door and kitchen streams connecting.

"But you *did* find my car out there," she said, exasperated now, "and you broke in the house anyway."

"I broke in *because* I found it."

"But that means you *knew* I'd be—" She stepped back, lost in the moment, then retreated from the spreading water to sit in the corner rocking chair, her knees up, feet off the floor.

He opened the door, letting several inches gush into the room, then stepped outside and held up the lamp. The door framed an unexpected scene, several trees all the way down, debris bobbing in the front yard, branches flying through the rain.

"Time to head up," he pronounced, rushing to the pantry to fill a sack with snacks and drinks from her fridge and cabinets. Setting their supplies on the stairs, he handed her the lamp, then started several times as if he would lift and carry her. Instead, he dragged her to the stairs, chair and all, so she could step up. "Water's cold; better stay dry."

They hustled their cargo up to the front bedroom. She set the rifle aside and perched on the bed while he pushed a cedar chest over to the window where he could watch the rising water.

Quietly, she asked, "Is this bad as it'll get?"

"Water's already topping the dam. Ground around it gives way, a whole lot more water's coming through here in a hurry."

"Will that pull down the house?"

He bit his lip, then cautioned, "We're not in the main channel, so I'm more worried about what's *in* the water. Floating trees and what-all push up against the house, that's a lot of push."

As if his words vibrated the very earth, a sustained rumble rose in the distance, echoing thunder growing louder and lasting too long.

Soon a higher-pitched roar overpowered it, drowning even the tin-roof onslaught.

The entire house groaned, following that with several shudders and loud bangs. It sounded like a mountain slamming into the walls.

She hobbled to the window, steadied herself against his shoulder, and watched the lamp's glow highlight the churning water now rising faster.

He hurried to look down the stairs and blurted, "Oh God." He yanked down the attic access and unfolded the wooden ladder steps, then helped her climb. He handed up the food bags, then bedspreads and sheets. By the time he joined her, the second floor had disappeared under several inches of brown water.

"Hurry!" she warned. "Pull up the stairs!"

"No, no," he said. "If water's coming anyway, don't make it come all at once."

And come, it did, an inch at a time over the next forty minutes, finally leveling out five steps from the top. Another half hour of sitting on each side to stare into the watery hole, and they seemed to hold back the flood by sheer will alone.

The lamp guttered again. "You got matches to re-light it?" he asked.

She pulled some from her pocket, agreeing they should preserve their oil. Once he extinguished the flame, darkness closed in around them. Neither said much beyond, "You hear that? What's that?" She thought of so many things to say, but never found the words. They stared toward each other, blind yet somehow unraveling twisted truths, and still she couldn't even recall his name.

Finally, he broke the spell. "How come you to be such a hater? And how come you's all alone out here?"

The pain washed over her again, weighing her down. She never told anybody her business, but words in the darkness didn't seem meant for anyone in particular. "They killed my Harold." She paused, and he said nothing, refusing to help, the work now hers and hers alone. "We'd been living in Detroit 'cause Harold worked at the Cadillac plant on

Clark, but we had just got us a house in the suburbs. 1967, hot hot summertime, and what broke loose in Detroit they hadn't started calling a riot yet. When Harold got off work he drove down Hastings to get Emma, the old woman who used to babysit when Cynth was little. He was gonna bring her out to our place till the trouble passed, but he never got to her." Tears filled her eyes again, and her voice broke. "Found him bludgeoned, they said. Blamed the rioters, but Emma said out her window she could see uniforms swinging billy clubs. Ain't nobody did a proper investigation." She wiped her eyes, her nose. "Ain't nobody cared."

A new wave of rain pounded the tin roof even harder, then eased up after a few minutes.

"Where's your daughter?" he said quietly.

Iris took a deep breath and sighed. "Twenty-four, pretty as a peach, engaged to be married . . . she stopped beside the road to help someone broke down. A car skidded into the whole mess, run her down—run her—" She cried openly now, that image she'd avoided picturing for decades begging to be seen, the infinite blackness now a velvet canvas on which to paint truth. "Took off, left her to die right there in the road."

"Oh damn," he said quietly, a voice in the dark. "I'm sorry."

"Sorry nothing!" she snapped. "Ain't *your* fault."

"Not *yours*, neither."

"Ain't nobody gives a damn anymore."

"Mamaw did," he insisted.

She buried her face in her hands, his words too true.

After a few minutes, he said, "I better check the water." He felt for her hand, then gently opened her fist and took the matches. The lamp revealed water at the top step inching its way higher. "It's time," he said.

He set the lamp in the middle of the floor, moved the groceries over by the window, and punched the transom several times to unstick the seal so he could slide up the single small pane of their dormer escape. As the roar of relentless rain filled the cramped space, he raced around, looking for supplies, not very pleased with what he found. An old wardrobe held some dry-cleaning, fancy dresses not much use in a flood. He carefully removed the fragile plastic coverings, thin veneers over a discarded past. In the bottom he found old winter clothes, including sweatpants and -shirts, and more sheets . . .

And an old, hand-carved box, the coin box.

Now she remembered.

"Put these on, quick," he said, giving her a set of sweats, then pulling a shirt over his tee. He set the coin box by the window, but never said a word about it.

Water crept across the unvarnished wood floor. He tipped the wardrobe on its side with a crash, then shoved it in front of the window. "Get up here," he urged, still trying to keep her dry. He carefully widened the hole in one plastic cover, had her step into it, and pulled it up like a long skirt, tucking it into her waistband. He tore two arm-holes and a head-hole in another, pulling it over her shoulders, tucking in a third to act as a hood. He repeated the process for himself, then shouldered the blankets and sheets, grabbed the coin box, and climbed out on the roof. "Hold the light out where I can see!"

She braced her good leg and leaned out the window with the lamp.

Slipping several times on the slick corrugated tin, denuded by rain, he set the coin box atop the dormer, then climbed up and threw blankets over the apex. He tied several sheets together, anchoring them to the chimney. Back inside, he crouched with her on the ward-robe, watching the water until it reached for their toes. Hooking the lamp just under the dormer eaves, he climbed out on the roof, then guided her out, putting a twisted sheet into her hands, helping her climb to the top. The blankets provided non-slip footing, a bit of cushion. Bracing her against the chimney, he tied one sheet into a loose sling.

"I don't want to trap us!" he shouted, his face against hers. "Put your weight into it, but if the house gives way, pull free and push off.

We get pulled apart, swim for something big. If it feels solid, like a tree, get up out of the water fast."

She trembled too violently to hold on, but he settled in beside her, put his arm around her, and held firmly. After a minute, she rested her head against his chest, feeling his warmth even as cold rain washed over them.

They couldn't see the lamp directly, but its glow across the water helped them monitor the rise. Eventually, they shifted around, finding a more comfortable position, still eyeing the water, now over the eaves and inching up the tin roof, just a few feet below them.

They wouldn't make it, despite all this. Nothing could save them now. If they wound up in the water and Caroline's boy tried to help, she would pull away, improve his chances without her.

Nearly submerged now, the lamp flickered and went out.

Black rain slapped at them furiously, testing their resolve. Sometimes people have no choice but to endure.

"They brought him inside," she said, crying now, picturing the image again for the first time in forty-odd years.

"Who?"

"Harold. Emma's neighbors. A couple risked their lives, grabbed him, carried him to their apartment, tried to help, called for an ambulance. Of course, none came."

"Most people's good," he said, "given a chance."

"And them two boys," she said, trying to catch her breath. "Two boys on their bikes, they stopped and stayed with my girl. One put his jacket over her, kept her warm while the other put his sweatshirt under her head. The man at the fire department told me about it when he come by with a card and some flowers from the squad. He cried a little when he give 'em to me, said it's hard answering a call like that, said if I needed anything . . ."

He pulled her closer, Caroline's boy, Caroline's grandson—called himself Edwin, she remembered now. Edwin held her tight, a selfless gesture, connection.

"Lotta people said the same thing, brought food, come by to help, neighbor kids mowing the grass . . . I figured they did that to make themselves feel better."

"They did it for you," Edwin said. "You just didn't notice, is all."

"I don't like to scratch the surface, see what's underneath, always expecting something bad, ugly."

Water touched their feet, and for some reason it felt good, knowing the time had come, the way, not feeling so alone.

Secret panel left open, Iris's submerged hidey-hole mocked her fears.

Trigger never pulled, Daddy's rusting rifle protected none from her fate.

Scattered by currents, Granddaddy's coins would sink forever in the river's mud . . .

But the water pulled back, dropping a few inches. The rain tapered off, turned to mist, then sputtered out.

In time, dawn broke over the horizon, misty patches of brightness peeking through ragged trees. The water had fallen to just below the eaves, a soggy hand-carved box holding fast.

Soon, a helicopter appeared, circled, and hovered. Sheriff Dander leaned out to check on them, signaling won't be long just hold on we're coming to get you.

The rumble of a speedboat approached from downstream. Sunbeams burst across the treetops, firing the revelation of one very different world emerging from receding waters, a world caked with mud yet somehow scrubbed clean.

The need to protect themselves past, two survivors huddling atop an old two-storey tin-roofer tore off their makeshift veneers and prepared to face a new day.

Lunatic

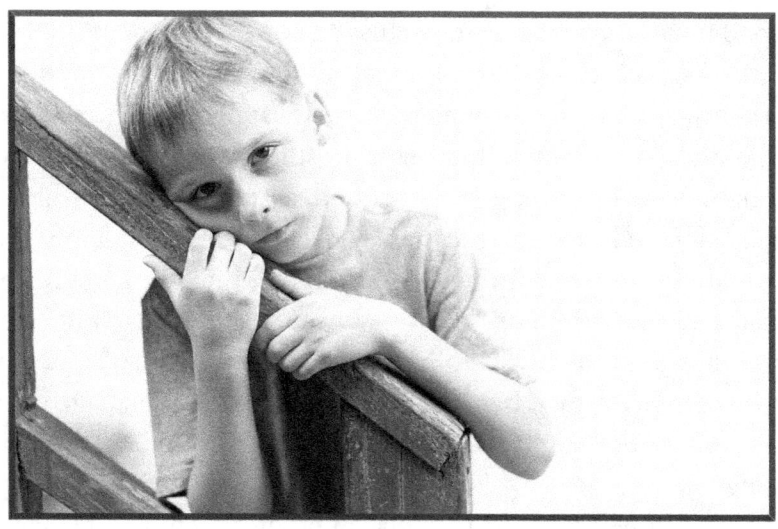

I thought about this as a youngster, but never considered it a story. Decades later I talked to an old man who'd had just such a friend as a lad, so I decided to write it for a website. Normally a short story offers the point of view of one or two characters, but I thought I'd try letting a character give that POV to something else. Every time I publish this somewhere, I hear from someone(s) recalling a similar experience. You're never too old . . .

In a world of gods and monsters, I've been called both, but no matter how many people watch me, there's a secret nobody knows:

I'm stalking a little boy.

His dad refers to him as Billy, but his mom sometimes calls him "My Big Boy," especially since he started school last year, though he's really not very big compared to others his age.

I admit our relationship is unorthodox, but even though I never intended it to happen, he seems to like having me around. Still, I try to keep my distance, but I do find myself following him, no matter how long the trip. When he's playing outside, I watch over him, sometimes even boldly showing myself, though mostly I stay hidden from view. Even then, he seems to know I'm around, and he counts on that.

Billy does talk to me, but only when he's alone at night in his room, whispering to me through the window. When he spies me peering inside, it cheers him up. He wipes away his tears to tell me stories, imagining the fun he hopes to have this summer, or maybe next year, or even when he really is big someday. Then if he does manage to sleep, I know I've helped him feel better. Still, I keep watching, often until morning.

Right now he's gone to that place he hates so much. I knew this would be one of those rough days when his mother laid out that outfit last night, including the cap he refuses to leave home without. He cried when he saw it, so she hugged him and called him her super-brave big boy, but he waited until she'd gone, then came to the window and whispered his fears to me again.

I can't be there for him today, though. I have places to go, things to do. I'm going as fast as I can, trying to get back before Billy comes out. I want him to see me as I follow him all the way home, to know I'm lingering outside his window, even though it's from a safe distance.

Okay, I'm here now, and I see his mother's car, so they must still be inside. It's taking longer this time, and that scares me. He's never stayed this late. It's getting dark out.

These trips keep proving harder and harder on him.

Most of the time I feel big and powerful, like I can shape the very world, lift oceans, guide lost souls . . . yet at times like this I feel utterly helpless. I can't save a frightened little boy who wears a cap because he's embarrassed about those treatments robbing him of every last lock of his soft brown curls.

Two nights ago, there from his window during our secret, special time together, he told me the silliest story. He spoke of frenzied objects dashing about, loony farm animals leaping into the air, some feline performing music, and he even gave me a part in his wonderful tale. He actually smiled as he told it, one of those increasingly rare moments when joy dances in his little eyes.

Ah, they're coming out now.

Oh no, he looks sick again. His mommy puts his cap on him, then picks him up and carries him to the car. He looks for me, and when he finds me I smile back, putting on my best face.

Tonight, this night, I dare to give him a reassuring wink.

So I follow him home again, a journey I've taken many times. I wait patiently outside during his bath time, his futile attempts to keep down a snack, the sickness. Finally, he's in bed now, but tonight he's moving about, uncomfortable. At least he seems to be managing some sleep. He needs the rest.

I'll wait out here as long as I can, peeping secretly through the window, a crazed lunatic watching one big little boy who needs a friend he knows will always come around.

I would bend the world for him. I would lift oceans. I would cast light into darkness. Were there any chance it might make him feel even the slightest bit better, I would hold still and let that loony cow from his story jump over me again and again.

Then, finally, Billy would laugh once more while that cat plays fiddle, a little dog laughs, and the dish runs away with the spoon.

Attention Pay

Sometimes it's heartbreaking, how much we can lose. Of course, that's when you can look more clearly at what's left. Might as well see it in the present tense and let thoughts run together, as they've been known to do. I hold a certain affection for Jimmy, and though he's entirely fictional, I liked spending this time with him.

A smart young man who knows the words but struggles to pay attention sits on his boardwalk bench, salty sea breeze swirling around him, the ice cream of his sugar-cone melting in the warm Florida sunlight.

And he cries.

His routine etching deep grooves through simple days, Jimmy has learned to find near-contentment in the markers of predictable moments reliably reminding him what must come next. A beeping alarm always means bedspread toilet shower clothing door-lock bike boardwalk donut-stand work. Tourists at the bike-rental counter mean half-day or whole-day ID credit card sign here. Owner Willie reminds him when it's time to pick up their lunch at Chick-On-Stick, then at 6:00 time to quit for the day. "Don't forget to stop for ice cream," adds the skinny old bike-rental owner, his face a totem of ridges and wrinkles tanned to the color of finger-burnished pennies. Willie never says much more than that, preferring to sit on his stool and pay attention to everyone and everything happening on the boardwalk.

An evening ice cream from Maureen's stand, then a seat on his favorite bench with plenty of time to eat it—that used to be the best part of Jimmy's day, certainly nothing to cry about. Then two months and three days ago Lila came to work for Maureen, and that complicated everything.

A voluntary resident at the group home two blocks behind the bluff, Lila introduced herself to Jimmy her first day on the job, then boldly declared, "I'm high-function special needs." Jimmy soon learned those are about the biggest words she knows, but her ideas often prove bigger than words, and by gosh she sure does know how to pay attention to people. Willie once remarked that she's not much to look at, but Jimmy considers her quite pretty, indeed, and somehow she looks even more beautiful each day, a notion he finds himself paying quite a bit of attention to, even at the oddest times.

Used to be, he would choose a flavor for his daily double-dip cone as he walked to the stand, but lately he's been squandering those minutes wondering which outfit she might be wearing, which hints of color might adorn her eyelids and lips and nails. Sure enough, he finds himself at the counter, people waiting in line, and has no idea what to order. It's getting to where she just picks a flavor for him.

Somehow, she always knows exactly the one he wants.

That ugly spotty dog wanders down the beach, sniffing at tourists and wagging his tail. Some shoo him away; others pet him, offer a treat. The seagull squadron overhead swoops in to steal his morsels, always paying attention to where the food is stashed, noticing coolers and baskets and sacks and pockets and little kids who might be startled into dropping their ice-cream cones.

Jimmy wipes the tears from his eyes and gazes down the boardwalk to where Lila works the counter. A slash of evening sunlight cuts through the interior gloom, making her glow and appear to be melting. That big guy with the dark bushy hair is still there, leaning on the counter, chatting up Lila and grinning incessantly. Jimmy always talks to her, but never for more than a few minutes because she has a job to do. She wants to save up to move someplace where nobody uses or breaks or steals her things. Yes, Jimmy has been paying attention.

It's not right that the grinning man doesn't buy ice cream. He probably doesn't even know how to eat it. Gobble it too fast, and you get *brain freeze!* Wait too long, and it melts all over your hand, even your clothes. Ice cream is a commitment, best savored as a perfectly timed indulgence, each layer opening itself to infinitely exquisite possibilities in the instant it melts. No wonder Jimmy always fits a daily cone into the routine of deep grooves etched through simple days.

The buckle on his sandal is coming loose. He spends too long puzzling over what to do about it, but he is distracted because that big bushy-haired guy is still down at the ice-cream stand. Jimmy refuses to let the frustration make him cry again, but seeing him talking to Lila is more than he can take. The view from his bench is ruined now, and it's too early to head home to his two-room apartment up Bleser Lane, so he has no choice but to give up his bench time today.

Opting to go on foot, he stomps his way along the boardwalk, then heads up the access trail behind the beach and finds himself wandering down a familiar sidestreet where the ramps and concrete steps are lined with lots of steel rails, all leading to houses up the rise. He used to skateboard here, doing tricks and impressing his friends, a smart foster boy living with the Jenkins family in their ramshackle house behind the bluff.

It happened at age fifteen, Jimmy a tenth-grader, almost six years ago. Somebody stole his helmet, and Mrs. Jenkins refused to get him another, so he went boarding without protection. He took that rail right over there, down along the concrete steps, then jumped to the curb, showing off for some girls watching from the street.

But he paid too much attention to the girls, not enough to the street.

All that time in hospitals, five operations, the state rehab facility, therapists insisting he might still be smart if he would just learn to pay attention, Mrs. Jenkins refused to take him back he's not right he could be dangerous just look at him . . . yet now he wants to show this awful place to Lila, to lay bare the connection between a future he wanted and the life he now lives. Maybe then she'll understand why nothing is where it needs to be until he finds the right way to fit it in, to link it to what comes before and after, each day a near-contentment of recurring loop reminding him what comes next.

Except when it gets complicated.

Little Braeden comes coasting down the roadway on his bike. Jimmy tries not to pay him any attention, but every time he sees the sandy-haired ten-year-old he can't help but feel happy for a moment before the sadness reminds him those connections now hurt.

A foster placement who's been living with the Jenkins family since last year, Braeden used to come around the bike-rental and visit Jimmy, sometimes helping him clean the bikes and pump the tires and fix the chains. One day with Willie off running errands in town, he tried to tell Jimmy what happened that made him a foster boy, but he started crying, and Jimmy forgot to listen to the words because the tears made him just listen to how Braeden feels. What mattered right then was that Jimmy always paid attention.

Closer now, Braeden notices Jimmy standing awkwardly beside the road. The youngster nods as he coasts by, but quickly looks away, embarrassed.

One day the boy's friends saw him hanging out with that "retard" at the bike-rental, and they teased him. The few times Braeden came by after that, his eyes darted around to see who else might be paying attention, and he always left right away.

When Jimmy counted twenty-six days without seeing Braeden anywhere, he made the big mistake of riding his bike over to the Jenkins house and asking about him. Mrs. Jenkins got angry and told Jimmy to go away, then called the police, who came to Willie's shop the next day and told Jimmy he better stop paying attention to Braeden. Willie got mad about it, too, but not at Jimmy. "It's a messed-up world," he said, shaking his head before returning to his stool. He also missed Braeden coming around, the way the boy asked so many questions that Willie wound up talking more than he used to.

"You're a good guy," Braeden says, startling Jimmy, who hadn't realized the boy circled back and stopped in the middle of the road. Braeden eyes the crusted cone clutched in the man's hand, dried ice-cream drips coating his fingers. "Some kids was talkin' bad, is all— 'cause you act so weird."

The boy executes a couple of figure-eights in the street, and Jimmy pays very close attention because watching Braeden reminds him to have faith that hurts don't always have to break connections, that sometimes they're just stretched too thin to see for a while. Braeden must need more time to figure out where to fit in.

"Sorry," says the boy, stopping again.

"We're still friends," Jimmy says.

"Yeah," Braeden agrees. He stands on his pedals and races up the hill, out of sight.

Several cars drive by, each slowing to eye the man standing absently beside the road. Jimmy pays attention to everyone who stares, but that brings angry looks, and suddenly he panics for not knowing what comes next. Needing to pay attention to what he knows, he hurries along the road, follows the access trail, and traces the boardwalk route to his seat on the bench.

There's a mess on his hand, the cone glued to his fist, which means way too late to eat his ice cream. That grinning guy with the dark bushy hair is still leaning on the counter, but Lila is looking down the boardwalk, paying attention to Jimmy.

And that feels good.

She does that a lot lately, but maybe thinking about him complicates her routine, too, the same way Jimmy sometimes can't sleep at night, always thinking about her.

That ugly spotty dog wanders back up the beach, his squadron of gulls patrolling above, but Jimmy doesn't pay them much attention because he is walking up the boardwalk now toward the ice-cream stand. He will tell that man to leave so he can talk to Lila. He will punch him in the nose, if that's what it takes.

"Jimmy!" Lila blurts, eyeing the empty cone, the mess on his hand. "What are you *thinking?*"

"I'm thinking about *you*," he pronounces, ignoring the big guy glaring with that too-common you're-a-retard look on his face.

Lila grins, those beautiful eyes glistening, her color today hinting at lavender, or maybe fuchsia or some other word Jimmy knows but doesn't care to wonder right now. "Well, mister," she pronounces, "let's get you clean." She comes around from behind the counter and firmly takes Jimmy's arm.

The grinning guy stops grinning as Jimmy tells him, "You go home now."

"Yeah, Gus," Lila agrees, "I'm busy now." She leads Jimmy behind the stand where a short hose dribbles water into a bucket, then holds him tenderly while rinsing the goop from his hand. She moves even closer, hair touching his face, fragrance tickling his nose, her warmth taunting him as the sunshine melts and drips down their bodies . . . and she holds his hand long after the water scrubs it clean.

"Who is Gus?" Jimmy wonders.

"Oh, he just likes me, but I don't like him. He's too *pushy*."

"He acts like he's your boyfriend," Jimmy says, the unspoken concept of jealousy finding new meaning among his big words.

"I know—but he keeps talking till I get *brain freeze*," she says, giggling.

Jimmy laughs with her because he's paying attention to exactly what she means.

"Lila," Maureen says, peeking out the back window with a knowing smile, "why don't you knock off early and have some ice cream with your friend down there on the bench?"

Lila shoos Jimmy toward his familiar spot, promising she'll come in a few minutes.

As he waits, that ugly spotty dog wandering the beach could very well turn into a horse, his squadron of gulls into pterodactyls; the boards in the walk could turn to snakes, the sky into streaks of lavender and fuchsia . . . Jimmy would never even notice because this smart young man who knows the words has something more important on his mind.

And when Lila joins him on the bench, she's holding two plastic dishes with upside-down ice-cream cones. "I like my ice cream this way," she announces, "'cause then I can take my time."

Jimmy finds himself thrilled by the very notion that he keeps knowing precisely what she means. Sampling the chilly confection, he says, "Hey, this is exactly the flavor I want."

She smiles and waits for him to spoon another bite before tasting a bit of her own. After several minutes of both taking their time, she pauses and looks serious, then leans closer to whisper, "I saw you crying, Jimmy."

"I thought you picked Gus," he says, a hint of sadness drifting by, then moving on, no place for it to connect.

Now Lila's eyes fill with tears. "I just thought Gus would make you hurry up."

"But you really picked me," he said, forgetting to listen to her words because the tears made him just listen to how Lila feels. "Gus doesn't fit in."

She puts her arms around him, and he holds her like no other can possibly exist in the world.

It seems that love is a commitment, best savored as a perfectly timed indulgence, each heart opening itself to infinitely exquisite possibilities in the instant it melts.

Maybe now a beeping alarm means bedspread toilet shower clothing door-lock bike *group-home Lila* boardwalk donut-stand *ice-cream stand* work . . .

She whispers, "I like how you eat ice cream," proving a good-hearted soul who doesn't know big words can be very smart, indeed.

"I like how you're not afraid of letting it get mushy," Jimmy declares. "Maybe we can try mixing two flavors together!"

They both laugh at the very idea, which proves that even a smart soul who knows big words really can find the most remarkable reason to pay attention.

Halfway House

Some debts, you can never discharge, yet many people keep making those payments. An allegory bigger than any one man's situation, this story resonates with me because I've always been fascinated by how people live. We always have choices. Too bad we so rarely take charge long enough to make them.

This guy's not all there, Freida thought, watching that felon his first day on the job. Named Connor, he seemed at times to drift away in his mind, his hands working without him.

The following week, he startled her in the big greenhouse, holding a long knife—caressing it, really—as if he wanted to cut someone, or maybe he already had.

He looked right at her a few days later. Caught, he glanced elsewhere, but surely he'd been imagining her, clothing torn away, body restrained, eyes confirming terror.

As Freida locked the florist shop one Friday, he hurried through the parking lot to catch his bus, but he slowed as he passed her clunky car, blatantly scanning the interior for steal-worthies, that fuzzy froggy dangling from her mirror not worth the explosive cacophony of breaking glass.

Soon after, he carried a huge clay pot to a customer's car, then waited patiently while the woman lit a cigarette before opening the trunk. He eyed the flame, more than enough to torch a block of row houses, wailing families trapped, helpless babies dying in the cinders.

Then ditzy Jenny returned from maternity leave after squeezing out her second bawler for Grandma to help raise. She reclaimed her counter job, and Freida found herself down-laddered to the greenhouses where Connor labored silently, his every moment GPS-tracked. Small assurance; once his rampage is over, the damage done, they'll have a printout showing he was there.

As he wrestled bags of Sphagnum onto a rack, he looked surprisingly small, his arms skinny. His sweep of sandy hair suggested innocent boyishness, though she would guess him to be about her age, low thirties, if that. Still, image deceives, and two halves dwell as opposite sides in the heart of every man. The most dangerous souls live in the side where it's darkest.

Freida's ex-fiancé had taught her this, tricking and conning his way into and out of her life, duping and hurting her until she'd grown weary of searching out the good. He'd left her with nothing, her reliable car stolen and crashed, modest home foreclosed, tuition unpaid and student loans due. An unwelcome occupier of her mom's dignity-squeezing apartment, gasping from the stench of an aging middle-ager's bitter depression, Freida escaped to toil by day among vast arrays of exquisite flowers, determined to coax the bloom of happiness from a life ground to dirt.

The Bernies had whispered about a halfway house. Could Connor escape into flowers, too? Or must he flee further than a mind can fathom?

"Yes, ma'am, I can," Connor was telling their bee-yotch boss, who stomped away in disappointment, missing that chance to remind a man of his limitations, his restrictions.

"No way," Freida warned him, ignoring her cautions enough to move closer, but not too. "*Eighty* more flats—by five-thirty?"

"By seven," he said, finding her eyes before looking away. "I moved. Only one bus now."

"Get out of here!" she said, handing him another bag of granules, which he poured into the sprayer's tank. Tendrils of hanging-pot vinery reached out to tickle their hair, stirred by the greenhouse vent-blower breeze.

"Freida!" shouted the bee-yotch from somewhere in the jungle. "You better help, too! Don't let our criminal miss curfew!"

From an aisle of trayed cuttings, Bernie the Younger paused his spraying to shoot a sneering grin their way. Working across from him, Bernie the Older scowled and waved his half-wit son back to the task.

Freida retrieved stacks of trays while he wheelbarrowed more medium inside. They developed a sort of assembly line, the only sounds a *whoosh* from the blowers and *coos* from mourning doves nesting among the lilacs just outside. His face blanked again, his movements suggesting a trance, a disconnect from anything not flowing through his hands, except that he did surface occasionally to check his watch before sinking back into the current of his efforts.

He was definitely not all there.

The electronic box in his fanny pack beeped. He started, an instant of apprehension, awareness of her curious presence, embarrassment, frustration, chagrin. It beeped several more times before he could loose the pouch, unzip it, and reach in to manipulate his tormentor. As the prompt grew more urgent, the Bernies paused to watch. The bee-yotch yelled, "Add another sixty to that order!" Connor knelt and checked something strapped above his ankle, then hurried outside. He returned after a moment, the pack silent, that chaperon riding his tail once again poised to squall. He set back to the task, increasing his pace.

"We won't be done by seven," Freida said.

He eyed her suspiciously, then looked away, thinking, weighing. "She wants to fire me," he said, setting down his trowel and bowing his head.

"But she *hired* you, so—"

He shook his head. "Old Man Brentwick did—for the tax credits." He picked up the trowel and started filling a tray.

"Can't you call the halfway house and get more time?"

His face hinted at a wince. He shook his head again, this time refusing to make eye contact. She'd managed to coax the skittish little jailbird to perch on her finger, but then she'd scared him away.

But he came back. "I live on my own now, eight o'clock curfew."

Sure, and on his own he lived every minute feeding himself to that parasitic tick of a GPS unit whose jaws burrowed into his butt.

At nearly seven o'clock it grew clear they would need another half hour. She could offer to stay and finish without him, but his failure might delight the bee-yotch, their common enemy.

"How far by car to your place?" she asked.

He lost himself in calculations for a moment, then decided, "Ten minutes."

"I'll drop you off," she pronounced, no discussion required, just like that, inviting the murderous raping counterfeiting thieving arsonist to direct her down some dark, secluded dead-end road.

Apprehensive, she drove too fast, arriving in eight minutes, half an hour to spare. He resided at the end of a gravel road surrounded by fallow fields, in a side-by-side duplex, its lived-in left-side unit neat and quaint and homey, the vacant right-side unit damaged, decrepit, and decayed. As he stepped from her car, she worried he might actually be so rude as to invite her in, daring her to find some polite way to decline, but he simply thanked her and allowed as how he would look forward to seeing her again tomorrow. He didn't even invite her in. How rude.

He turned to walk up the steps, but hesitated and looked back.

"I'm waiting until you *get in*," she admonished. Silly man, no social graces, probably not all there.

And he went to the door on the right! He let himself in, *waved bye*, and disappeared inside.

Five weeks, she dropped him off every evening. It annoyed her at first, then downright pissed her off that his side of the duplex never seemed to improve. She could see not investing in the structure for the landlord, but he could have cleaned it, fixed it up, taken some pride in the appearance of his home. After he'd festered so long in prison, didn't finally having a real place to live mean something?

On the job, he avoided talking, something about appearing to have anything to do with anybody inexplicably making him nervous, but he usually relaxed a bit in the car afterwards, talking some, though never much. He worried constantly, this grew clear—about his pages-long list of ridiculous restrictions, about losing his job, about everything and nothing in a life that eventually inevitably goes wrong.

Finally on a day when they had time to spare, she stopped at a small grocery and announced, "You're inviting me in tonight, and I'm bringing the food and drinks."

He followed her inside, up and down the aisles, nodding and shaking his head, maybe even amused by her barrage of queries as she bustled about. Yes, he does have a stove, cookware, fridge . . . cleaning supplies. "I'm serious," she said. "I need to feel, um . . . *comfortable*." That embarrassed him, as did having to emphatically say no when she gestured toward beer and wine. Oh yeah, that pages-long list of ridiculous restrictions . . . "Is the bathroom clean?" she asked, skeptical of his nod, but trying not to show it. She felt bad about riding him so, but if a guy can't learn in prison how to take some upside-yo-head, then where's he *ever* gonna learn it?

And what's with this being afraid all the time? Weren't there bigger things to be scared of in the joint than out here on the streets? The living area looked awful, piles of junk everywhere, towels and sheets posing as curtains, flea-market rejects standing in for lamps; but the couch and low tables and older-model TV all looked immaculately clean—an odd contradiction, as if a man volunteering to live in hell nevertheless demands a relaxing place to sit.

She carried the food to the kitchen, again finding that disconnect where broken drawers and splintered cabinets prove spotless, the plumbing and sink scrubbed to a sparkle. She invited herself to wander back through the dining area, poked her head into a meticulous bathroom, and found three bedrooms, the open one neat and clean, the other two closed. She reached for the first knob, and he didn't object, so she peered inside to find dusty piles of junk, then checked the other and found a similar rat's nest. Well, one could certainly tell which of three cells belonged to *this* con.

She poured them some cold sodas, then set about frying sirloin tips and simmering a saucy vegetable medley. He hovered around, offering to help, following orders, setting a surprisingly beautiful table complete with wildflower bouquet, and he seemed to be thoroughly enjoying himself, though in an awkward, still-skittish way.

He *is* all there, just needing a reason to *reveal* the rest.

They ate in front of the TV, shouting out *Jeopardy* answers, teasing each other about unexpected expertise in the oddest categories. She regaled him with crazy-customer anecdotes from her time at the florist's counter, and he uncaged some wacky prison tales—apparently sometimes funny things actually happen in the joint. He placed his electronic box in its cradle right at eight, then recalled several embarrassing encounters he'd suffered as a result of its penchant to beepingly demand attention for no reason at all. Several times she pondered *the big question*, but always decided maybe she'd rather not know. Finally, she settled for going halfway there: "Look, I just want to know two things."

He picked at a loose thread hanging from his shirt button.

"Were you guilty?"

He nodded. "Yes."

"Any chance you would ever do it again?"

He shook his head. "None."

That first night, she kissed him on the cheek as she left. The second, he kissed her back. In the coming weeks, their exchanges expressed slowly increasing passion. As she felt more at home, and he grew more accustomed to her barging intrusion, she pressed her preference to see the place, you know, *fixed up*.

"And how come I never see the people next door?" she wondered one evening.

"Nobody lives there."

"Really?" She headed out to the porch, Connor right behind. "It looks so—

" She peered through the window, then worked her way around the side, standing tiptoe for curtain-peeps. Fully furnished, it boasted beautifully crafted furniture. Posing on the walls, landscape paintings and photographs modeled their fine formal frames. An exquisitely carved fireplace mantle flaunted its constant charms, unthreatened by the notion of ephemeral flames flaring up to wave for attention. The dining-room set displayed its mahogany pedigree, polished to a sheen, while the staid kitchen cabinetry lent gravitas to a domain any Food Channel chef would covet. Some sort of flat-roofed out-building squatted forlornly in the tall grass out back, the path to its door long-since ceded to weeds. She peered into the duplex's rear windows. Three bedrooms waited patiently, one a playland for the little girl who arranged her unicorns and dolls on shelves built into a princess castle; one a swirl of baby-boy blue staging an antiqued crib for the royal prince; the biggest a king-and-queen's boudoir, oakenly solid for the family man, frilly and soft for his beloved bride and mom to their kids.

"It's furnished!" she announced, even as he glanced about nervously and urged her back inside. "And clean, too," she added just as a black cop-car-styled sedan pulled up in front.

"My parole officer," he whispered, rushing her toward the porch to meet a tan-skinned Shrek in leather jacket and ill-fitting polyester slacks. His black slick-back hair and bushy 'stache stereotyped some-thing, but she couldn't quite place what.

"Who's this?" he demanded, not waiting for an answer, which Connor couldn't explain anyway. "And where were you?"

Freida tried to tell him, but he barged into Connor's place and stomped around, opening drawers, tossing cushions, popping a whole cookie into his mouth.

She offered, "I'm thinking of renting the place next door."

"Right," said the PO, adding a snort as he inspected the tether box in its cradle on his way out. He drove off in a cloud of road dust.

"So," she said as Connor dropped onto the couch, unsettled, "what happened to the family next door?"

He hesitated. "Killed—by a drunk driver, is what I heard. Don't know the details."

"You should talk to the landlord about moving over there."

He shook his head, then headed for the kitchen. "No one can move in there—yet."

So they ate, watched television, and held hands for a while. Get-ting up to leave, she suggested they make plans for their upcoming day off.

"I can't," he said. "Parole office, then errands, too much . . ." He sighed, weary, frustrated—she could only guess.

"I could go with you," she offered, "drive, at least—wait in the car."

He searched her eyes, and seemed about to say yes, but he looked away, his shoulders sagging. "Stuff I need to do myself."

"Okay," she said, putting her arms around him. "I could be waiting for you when you get back."

And he smiled. He hadn't forgotten how, after all. Or maybe he had, but just now finally remembered. He fished around in his pocket and produced a shiny key, so new its edges virtually growled as it bared its teeth.

She never left that night, and though they slept little, all fumbling and nervous, they eventually found each other, and for the first time in her life she saw that what just happens to happen can prove way more interesting than what anybody intends to happen.

"I'll be here when you get home," she promised the next morning, planning a day of cleaning and organizing. She dropped him at the bus stop, then headed out to fill her trunk with supplies, intending to turn half a house into a whole home.

She quickly found the task daunting. Too much and too many crammed the corners, stacked the shelves, piled the floors. She hauled the apparent disposables and unreclaimables out to the road, but a lot could prove useful: building supplies, tools, fittings, fixtures, and pristine rugs. She headed to the outbuilding to look for storage space, but found the door locked. Dusty windows revealed shed-style storage at one end—yard equipment, riding mower, a little girl's bike—with the bulk of the floorspace arranged as a wood shop: all manner of saws, a monster lathe, racks of tools, and lots of gear she didn't recognize. They had been remodeling the place themselves . . .

The dead family.

Fixing up the other side, they had barely begun phase two of an unlived life, maybe as income property, or space for friends, extended family.

Freida spent hours dragging and piling and cleaning, filling the two extra bedrooms to the ceiling, then filled a notepad with intentions: measurements for curtains, lists of repairs, needed supplies and linens and fodder for the cupboard . . .

Over the next few weeks, the place brightened more with every accomplishment. They worked together, learning each other's rhythm and style, his skills and artistry blooming. Still, sometimes it seemed she would lose a piece of him, especially when he sat in silence, or gazed out the window. She woke one morning and found him in the yard staring across the field beyond the outbuilding.

On their days off, she would coax him to go out, see a movie, picnic in the park, browse the big-box store. He always stayed close to her, nervously protective, self-conscious about his electronics, embarrassed by unprovoked beeps, and looking quite relieved to arrive home.

Then one morning she presented him his own set of keys to her car and asked him to run to the store.

"I—I can't," he said, shock in his face as he quickly handed them back. "No license, suspended for life."

And then she saw the awful truth.

She took his hands, felt him trembling, searched his eyes. "It was you."

His eyes filled with tears.

"You were the drunk driver who killed that family."

His lip trembled, and a tear spilled down one cheek. He slowly nodded.

"Oh God. A little girl . . . That baby boy . . ."

"No baby yet," he said. "They were rushing to the hospital, too fast, too dark."

And a drunk driver lurked out there in the night. "And you don't even remember it."

He shook his head. "What they told me. Pleaded guilty. Deserved worse."

Tears spilled from her eyes, and she held him close, both trembling now. She knew he would never mean to hurt someone. But how could he learn to live with the awful truth, an entire family gone, their home empty, their lives unlived?

They moved to the couch, rubbed each other's shoulders, wiped their faces. She wondered, "How can you live here—I mean, so close?"

"No place else to go," he said, and though surely other places waited nearby, she thought maybe he needed to see the result, to feel the absence, to know the truth of an instant he might never remember.

It took some time to find each other that night, and they woke exhausted before heading to the greenhouses. Freida pulled counter duty to cover for Jenny again.

"I'm leaving early," Jenny said, her grin announcing good news. "I'm getting married!" she squealed. Both women jumped around and hugged each other. "It's that guy—Carlo? I told you about him? Makes good money working for his dad? We're going to Vegas, then looking for a place for us and the kids."

As Jenny bustled about, waiting for her ride, Freida pondered the stark comparison between how one family can blossom while another just disappears in an instant of horrible mistake, and she wished Jenny the best, a chance at finally finding what she'd searched for in so many wrong directions. "Hey, I might know a place for you," she told them when Carlo came to whisk her away. "I'll look into it while you're gone."

And she did, using some downtime to search the county database for contact information on the duplex's new owner.

That evening she hugged Connor for a long time, then asked him for the key to the outbuilding in back.

His shoulders dropped, and he bowed his head. She knew he would have one. He took a deep breath, then reached for her hand and led. He stomped some of the tall grass to make it easier for her to get to the door, then slid his hand underneath the window ledge and produced the key. He looked at her, and where she expected suspicion, reticence, or at least confusion, she found relief. He rubbed his face and sighed.

"When?" he asked.

"Only this morning. I discovered you bought this building even before you went to prison. *You* were fixing this place up," she said, nodding toward the door. He opened it, and they stepped inside. "You finished the left side, then rented it to that family, but never got to finish the other."

They stood in the musty, dusty workshop where a whole man could build dreams.

"No," he said. "That's not what happened."

She took his hands and looked into his eyes, and this time he refused to look away.

"That little girl," he said, tears drawing lines to his chin, "the little brother she never knew, their mama . . . they died because a stupid man convinced himself the baby wouldn't come early, because a fool thought he could drink that night and still keep his family safe."

"But how would you—?"

He shook his head. "Their daddy, their husband . . . he didn't die, didn't even get hurt. No, the price *he* paid is having to live with it."

And live with it, he did, for when a man's not all there, he must be somewhere. Maybe he has no place else to go, so he dwells on the other side.

But deserved or not, there always exists that glimmer of possibility that another beautiful soul will reach out, open the door, take down the towels and sheets, let in some light.

"For me?" she said after weeks had passed, watching him cut new cabinet doors.

"For us," he corrected, handing her the sander. "If you want."

"I want," she said, smoothing hard edges, learning how to join him in the safe place where he loses himself to work with his hands.

And the left side sang again with the laughter of Jenny's children and Carlo's love for his burgeoning family, while the right side gradually discovered how to realize its promise.

And when the parole officer barged inside, the man who lived there proudly said, "I'd like you to meet my wife."

And she would spend many hours learning about the people he'd loved and lost, and she would honor their memory, too.

And then one sunny day an expectant father carried an ornately carved and hand-built crib inside, and both halves of a house completed an exquisitely loving whole.

And in the years since, in those moments when it seemed the man wasn't all there, the woman who loved him knew exactly where to find him.

About Face

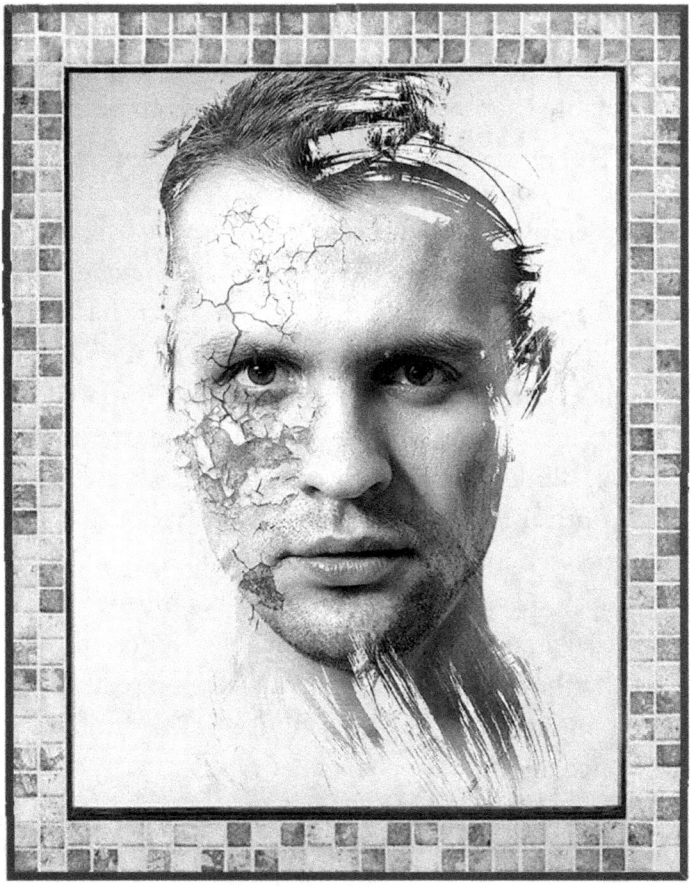

I like writing "slipstream," which is what we used to call a very real story about something that can't possibly be—or something like that. It's even more fun when the point is dressed up as a metaphor. Found myself in a mood for some faux-formal narrative. This what-would-you-do is an about-face for me—about face.

One particular Friday, a rather remarkable day, 34-year-old Jeremy P. Wilkins started the morning like he would any other: he looked himself in the face.

But this time someone entirely unfamiliar looked back.

Yes, it sounds rather fanciful, theoretically impossible, practically incomprehensible; but there staring at him from the mirror appeared the understandably stunned-looking mien of a complete stranger.

Now, being typical, Jeremy P. Wilkins immediately undertook a series of troubleshooting protocols similar to what any of us could be expected to employ, what we might call "reality checks." First, he touched the offending face and determined that he could feel it with his fingers and feel his fingers with the face. Then he examined the looking-glass itself and, having concluded it to be the same unaltered mirror that had never previously betrayed him, initiated a rigorous regimen of testing for some form of heretofore unexperienced abnormality of vision. Blinking several times, closing his eyes longer to initiate a form of optical reboot, rubbing vigorously, dousing thoroughly, and even alternately covering one eye at a time . . . all produced no change. A cursory survey of his environment confirmed the complete lack of other visual anomalies, so he quickly stripped off his clothing and conducted a thorough body inspection, both directly and by using the unreliable mirror, until he found himself forced to conclude that only his face appeared to have changed.

Seven mirrors, Jeremy P. Wilkins managed to locate in his modest apartment, not counting reflective surfaces such as the side of his toaster and the pane of glass fronting his microwave oven. All featured the same unfamiliar face, after which this thoroughly befuddled and, admittedly, rather alarmed young man briefly pondered, then discarded, the notion of religious significance. That left him considering the possibility that he suffered some sort of dysfunction with his mental faculties. What kinds of illness or intoxication, he wondered, might produce such a localized and limited distortion?

That quickly failed to yield meaningful results, so he decided to see if the appearance change could be detected by others. He found his elderly neighbor, Mrs. Rotwood, in the lobby, retrieving her mail from the key-boxes. Disguising his voice and adding a hint of non-specific accent, he made eye contact, then busied himself sifting through a stack of flyers on the bench as he casually greeted her by name.

"I'm sorry," said the surprised woman, pausing to peer at him. "Have we met?"

"You don't remember? We met last year?" He glanced at his watch, pronounced himself late, and mumbled apologies as he hurried out the door.

From across the street, he watched her dither a bit, perhaps lost in her own confusion, before she closed the key-box and disappeared upstairs, after which he slipped back up to his place and called his friend.

"It's my fault," Randall Q. Caruthers said so matter-of-factly that it startled his caller. "I caused it."

"I'm serious, man. My face really changed."

"I believe you. Happened to me, too. That's why I was off the grid last weekend. Pulled together some cash and drove to Atlantic City for three days of nobody-knows-your-name."

Now, what's remarkable about the subsequent exchange is that Jeremy P. Wilkins ultimately found himself accepting Randall Q. Caruthers's outlandish explanation, primarily for lack of any other, and because it did manage to account for the facts of the situation, facts that persisted as plainly as the nose on his new face.

It seems that Randall Q. Caruthers had received his own temporary face change from his brother-in-law. After three days the recipient's face reverts to his original, it was explained, and he is thereafter able—required, as it were—to pass that experience on to the first person whose face he touches. In this case, Randall Q. Caruthers had casually tweaked the nose of his friend, knowing full well that, several days hence, Jeremy P. Wilkins would wake to find a substantially altered visage peering back from his mirror.

"You're telling me," Jeremy P. Wilkins demanded, "that you looked like this for three days?"

"Well, no," his friend explained. "I'm told it's a different face every time. In fact, mine showed the rather pronounced characteristics of markedly different ethnicity."

Randall Q. Caruthers cut off the expected barrage of questions before it could even erupt, ending the conversation with one simple— if cryptic—admonition: "Look, just be careful, and since it's a one-shot deal, think big."

Think big, indeed.

Jeremy P. Wilkins started his *big* thinking with a rather *small* notion: not wanting to *explain* this face change to anyone. Thus, he concluded, he must miss a day of work before his customary two days off for the weekend. He called in sick to the dealership where he normally would have spent his day matching finance-approved buyers to the vehicle models and options that generated the best commissions.

The only salesman who routinely outsold him answered the phone. Augustus O. Crabtree barely concealed his delight over the pending absence of his chief competitor, which sparked two thoughts in the mind of Jeremy P. Wilkins: loss of a day's sales would put him further behind in their comparative monthly totals, and having a new face presented quite the unique opportunity to spy on the practices of his nemesis.

Thus, when an unfamiliar face walked into the dealership and approached the most aggressive salesman, Augustus O. Crabtree never suspected prior acquaintance. The "customer" fished a scrap of paper from his pocket and read off the name of the salesman to which he had been referred.

"No Wilkins here," Augustus O. Crabtree insisted, "but I can help you."

"No no," replied the customer. "I was told specifically to ask for Wilkins. My aunt bought a car from him years ago."

Thereafter followed a pitch that broke nearly all the dealership rules with its intent to steal the referral from—and tarnish the reputation of—another sales associate. Jeremy P. Wilkins left angry, but gratified to have surreptitiously recorded the exchange, which he might well use in several productive, even vindictive, ways.

Enjoying the possibilities of his new identity, he undertook to shop the competing dealership across the street, then several others in the area, always expressing a seller-challenging strong-but-swayable preference for the models sold at Jeremy P. Wilkins's place of employ. The lies, false promises, unsubstantiable claims, and unethical tactics he found so surprisingly prevalent at first shocked him, then stirred him to adopt a new outlook regarding his approach to the cutthroat field of vehicle sales.

Come Monday, Jeremy P. Wilkins might well expect to recover his customary face, but an important part of him likely would never be the same.

He sat in his modest apartment's dining area that Friday evening, failing to muster enthusiasm over his microwaved dinner of salisbury steak and vegetable medley, pondering how "loss of innocence," the stripping of one's practiced naïveté, can sow doubts in the fertile fields of imagination. This reminded him how he had long found vague discomfort in his girlfriend's insistence that he not show up at the rock-band lounge she assistant-managed, her busiest times Friday and Saturday nights.

"You won't like how I have to flirt with the customers for tips," she always explained, "especially when I work the bar."

He understood salesmanship, or so he thought, but here at home alone on yet another lonesome night, he found himself surprisingly curious about her boundaries. It comes as no surprise, then, that Jeremy P. Wilkins decided to take his unfamiliar face out drinking, a chance to observe his girlfriend's behavior without her suspecting his presence.

Five beers and several hours into the evening, what for a while appeared to be the kind of situation his girlfriend had always described, now started transforming into something entirely different. The man he'd noticed her smiling to in a store several weeks before—"He was in a class I took at the learning annex last year"—arrived to an overly friendly welcome. Situated at the end of the bar, he earned considerable attention from the assistant manager, and even managed to drink without paying. Twice, the man and assistant manager, hands all over each other, giggled and groped their way into the back office for brief periods; and when break time came, they left the premises together, looking very much a couple.

Jeremy P. Wilkins followed, dismayed to discover that they ventured no farther than a dark blue SUV parked in the back of the lot, its windows growing steamy within minutes. Impelled by anger, emboldened by his false face, he stumbled drunk-like past the vehicle. Surreptitious interior glances confirmed the worst. Come Monday, his original face intact, Jeremy P. Wilkins would undertake his extrication from any kind of personal relationship with such a two-faced so-and-so.

And in that knowledge, he found some measure of relief. It seems that even a hint of fear that monsters *might* lurk in the closet had proven more difficult to bear than obtaining proof that one does.

Thereafter, in the late hours of dark night, alone in his modest apartment, the story of Jeremy P. Wilkins's weekend of facing the truth took a very dark turn. Like some criminal on a burgeoning crime spree, he had tasted the sweet fruit of reaching beyond the fence with little risk of accountability. He sat on the side of his bed, the faint odor of discarded salisbury steak permeating the air, and considered the facts before him: he had two other-face days left, and there still existed in his small world one man he wanted very much to deal with, the one man he wanted very much to confront, the one man he wanted more than anything to see . . .

Dead.

And the more he thought about it, the more want became need.

Carl T. Tomlinson had persisted, a few years back, in the role of "boyfriend" to the younger sister of Jeremy P. Wilkins for approximately eleven months. In that time, the man's caustic style of interpersonal relations had grown increasingly violent. Why the young woman had kept the facts hidden from family and friends for so long, let alone put up with such abuse, proved beyond comprehension for Jeremy P. Wilkins and others close enough to care. Still, as the truth became more obvious, the man's methods of intimidation came to the front, and cooler heads conceded an inkling of understanding for her reticence, an inkling that nevertheless escaped the young woman's older brother.

By then, Carl T. Tomlinson had drained the young woman's life savings, totaled her car, trashed her modest home, and beaten her often enough and harshly enough to leave her dentally damaged, not to mention facially disfigured with a scar below her right eye. That she steadfastly refused to cooperate with any legal action testified to her fear of the man.

Jeremy P. Wilkins and his new face slept fitfully that Friday night, and rose early to plot the demise of Carl T. Tomlinson. He considered hundreds of details, then visited an internet cafe not too close to his modest apartment, logging on in a very public way to search details about the life of the object of his wrath.

He withdrew funds from his account in order to move about with cash. He purchased the smallest, most compact crossbow that would do the job, and quickly resurrected his college-team archery skills by repeatedly targeting an overstuffed chair in his modest apartment. He obtained accessories from rubber gloves to the face-concealing gear he would need during the later portion of his escape. He traced and retraced the routes, rehearsing every detail, then arranged transportation that allowed his car to remain visible in its customary spot at the modest apartment's garage.

On Sunday evening, with only hours remaining for him to possess an unaccountable face, he walked into the small convenience store where clerked Carl T. Tomlinson.

The man's current girlfriend lingered this side of the counter.

Careful to show his false-face to every obvious security camera, Jeremy P. Wilkins produced the small crossbow from under his jacket and ordered both to step behind the salty-snacks rack and fall to their knees. Speaking with his altered voice, he assured the young woman she would never be hurt—at least not by the intruder—then turned his attention to Carl T. Tomlinson.

Knowing he must accomplish his goal and escape quickly, Jeremy P. Wilkins promised the kneeling man that his days abusing and robbing women would end here and now, then lashed out with a kick to the face that sent him reeling, a pronounced gash on his cheek bleeding profusely. He lifted the crossbow and aimed . . .

And felt sick to his stomach, so sick that he risked vomiting DNA evidence all over the floor.

Jeremy P. Wilkins reeled at the notion of killing a man, and found that even the briefest outburst of violence had proven more than he could abide.

It seems that new faces are but masks, a means to pretend another, but they change not who we are.

"That'll leave a scar on your face to remind you I'm watching, and I'll be back," Jeremy P. Wilkins warned the man on the floor before beating his carefully rehearsed hasty retreat.

After sleeping fitfully again, Jeremy P. Wilkins rose exhausted, but raced to his bathroom mirror, relieved to find his familiar face back where it belonged. He studied it for several minutes, perhaps seeing it in new light, and realized he'd not preserved his own photographic evidence of the other face.

And with that he considered the notion that maybe, just maybe, it never happened, that maybe he had never foolishly allowed himself to indulge that which he might otherwise never dare face; but like legions before him, he avoided dwelling on the facts of his prior choices in order to focus, instead, on moving on.

He called his girlfriend to wish her many nights of happiness in the back of a dark blue SUV. At work, he advised the sales manager about his day-off silent-shopping expedition, then enjoyed a productive discussion devising counter-strategies. After pulling his chief competitor aside to hear the recording, then implying he also possessed evidence of illegal business practices, he managed to bluff and bully Augustus O. Crabtree into resigning his position.

Over the next few days, Jeremy P. Wilkins considered but failed to decide whose face he would touch, whom he would select to experience the gift and the curse of finally seeing oneself clearly. That gradually gave way to a bigger issue, though, the question of whether that unfamiliar face had merely risen from the ether of unexplainable mysteries; or if maybe, just maybe, it had otherwise belonged to *another* living soul.

He moved much closer to an answer later that week when he recognized the face of his friend, Randall Q. Caruthers, all over the news. It started with a montage of security-camera views showing him robbing banks and convenience stores and a bakery and hapless shoppers who had just withdrawn money from ATMs, all in upstate New York; then perp-walking in handcuffs, asserting his innocence while the news reporter countered that claims of spending the weekend in Atlantic City remained unsubstantiated.

And immediately Jeremy P. Wilkins realized that someone he never knew, someone he had briefly met only by face, would have borne full responsibility and suffered the severest consequences had plans of crossbow retribution been carried out.

And for many years thereafter, Jeremy P. Wilkins weighed the gravity of having assumed moral responsibility for protecting the reputation of another man's face.

And Jeremy P. Wilkins thereafter endeavored to conduct his affairs in a manner by which he could start each morning, well, facing himself in the mirror.

For you see, nothing makes a man appreciate the integrity of his own face like spending the rest of his life pondering three very remarkable days and wondering . . .

Just who did what with mine?

Holler Song

This piece is an example of narrative point-of-view. Although it's in the 3rd person (he, she, it), the narrator speaks somewhat the way a character would. Not just bad grammar on my part, that. Growing up in the snowy North, I looked forward to visiting my kinfolk in the hollers of Tennessee, not just for what they said, but for how they said it. Retta has a practical side you can't fault, especially that fluid morality it sometimes takes to live day to day.

*R*etta danced the willy-nilly, grabbed at slick branches, then lost both feet and whomped back-end down on the ice. Hit 'em mean like that and 70-year-old bones act scared, then angry, then out for revenge—and they'll complain bitterly for weeks. It's not how hard the ground is, makes 'em mad; it's how brittle the bones has got.

Now a sheet of frozen slick, this low patch in the double-rut drive-back had been needing some 'dozer work a long time running, one of many get-to's set for when next year's lump-sum money could hire some younger help. Hardly anyone drove it but Randall, easing the pickup 'tween overgrown mirror-snaggers when he brung groceries and what-not to Lurlene and her girl. Deputy Wallace used to ramble back here regular-like to pretend friendly and keep an eye for signs local cookers mighta set up, but when he found Hollis's makeshift lab a ways down Cutter Road, his brother Cletus shot him dead. State Police come in and tore 'em up from there to right up Middleton Holler just beyond. Now a new deputy's done took over, but ain't yet been out here lying about smells to claim "probable cause" when he trespasses on Lurlene and Retta's private property. This very minute would be a good time, him to show for a howdy-ma'am, seein' as how there's an old lady needs picking up off her arse.

Retta rolled over on her side and wound up mashing the holdin' end of that pocketed fish-knife into her thigh, then managed despite bad arthritis to pull herself up and set about shuffling forward, keeping to the treeline for more grab-branching. She came to sight of cousin Lurlene's place, built by their granddaddy when he carried his unimpressed young bride here for a lifetime of second thoughts in the hills of East Tennessee. Lately the place looked embarrassed at being let to run down, but now the dim gray fog and last night's snow gave it a fairy-tale gingerbread-house look, all sugar-frosted and gleaming with drips of icing drooping its eaves. Wisps of smoke fed by a stingy stack of splits curled from the chimney and bent north to tickle more sleet from dark clouds of a mind to paint these hollers another coat of quick-freeze.

Lurlene stepped out and stood on the wide, covered porch. Ten years younger than cousin Retta, she looked real old of a sudden. Bundled in wool coat, crochet hat and scarf, jeans and hide boots, she'd already got a mind to head out. "Found her, didn't they?" she asked as Retta stopped at the slicked-over bottom step. Eyes red and swole, Lurlene had been crying, imagining the worst and expecting nothing better.

Retta sighed and nodded. "TJ got eyes on her. Sykes Bluff, about like I figured."

Lurlene sagged terrible, legs about to give out, but she gripped the rail and held herself up.

"Randall and TJ done started on gettin' her up, gonna need our help," Retta said, looking off into the ice-gleaming woods. Seemed like she oughta be hearing one of those no-words nonsense songs scattered among the trees, but them days was gone.

Lurlene eased her sturdy frame down the slippery steps, then acted for a second or two like she might just hug her cousin's neck, but them days was gone, too. As a kid she'd hug the neck of anybody would let her, but not too many would, and the older cousin went from not too often to not for some time now. Hugs never much suited her or Randall, Retta's husband, who started coming around sparkin' when he and Retta was teenagers and li'l-dab Lurlene got just old enough to walk clear to her cousin's place at the high end of the holler. Turned out not to suit TJ much, neither, ever since Randall's grand-nephew come to visit and never left. Lurlene used to spend plenty of hugs on Frances, her only child, the girl Clayton left her to raise alone when he up and disappeared; then on Cammie, the chestnut-haired grandbaby she raised after a bullet shard behind the ear left baby-girl to grow up not caring if she ever got hugged or not, for all the good they woulda done. What'll Lurlene do now with all them hugs, and nobody to take 'em?

"Slippery uphill," Retta said, leading her through the woods to avoid the iced-over double-rut.

Not a hundred yards up yet, and both of Retta's bad hips demanded to know just where she thought to get to. "I reckon," she said, breathing hard already, "we best carry the girl straight to rest with her mom and them."

"No preacher? Nobody to come?"

Retta shook her head. "Can't even think about trying to show her face—" She stopped and turned. "'Sides, you let it be known she's dead, checks'll stop, and next year's big'n won't never come, neither."

Lurlene kept quiet, turned and looked away. The woods tinkled and popped, bits of ice falling, branches cracking, a beat with no song in it for singing. Mist skulked about, sniffing at all the shiny bark. Lurlene was showing that look on her face, the one where she's still picturing how it happened, bullets flying, newlyweds sprawled in a pool of blood, baby-girl wailing in dead mama's arms, daddy's shot-up body still holding the stick police tried to say looked like a gun. Lurlene had just convinced her daughter to move back this side of the state line, maybe even back to the holler, but family comin' home wound up two bodies for buryin' and six-month-old Cammie with the tip of her nose grazed, her brain messed up for good from that head wound. Time the lawyers got through, Cammie was set with a small monthly check barely paid for all the pills, plus a big lump sum to come next year on her 25th, supposed to last the rest of her life. Them pills made her okay to be around when the pain wasn't too bad. Sometimes her mind would focus just enough to care a bit about what-all is and where she fits into it. Those days, often as not, would find her somewhere by herself in the holler, singing, like that to be her only job in the world.

Retta stood there in the iced-over woods and waited for Lurlene to think her way back around to the job at hand. Mist crept closer, curious, sniffing their sleeves. Ice slid off a big branch not ten feet away, clattered and cracked its way into the brush. Seemed like Cammie oughta be out there singing right now, the way she'd find wannabe words in the tunes, no sense in 'em lest you knew how to listen to what she meant and not what she said. Retta thought she might could understand a time or two, but maybe not. Lurlene seemed to could make a bit of sense of her, and TJ turned out to have a knack. He could make her sit still long enough to look right at him, and lately he'd even figured how the right kinda look back could make her smile. Seemed like she finally understood something when she lit up like that. Everybody figured that to be a good thing, but after what she done last night, maybe not.

Maybe she finally understood too much.

Lurlene wiped her face with a sleeve, and they moved on without another word. Once they crested the rise and crossed the flat-top, they come to Randall belly-down and dangling blue rope off the overhang of creek-bluff. Lurlene stopped a dozen feet short, stood over by a tree where Randall's rifle and TJ's shotgun leaned, several coils of rope close to hand.

Randall turned and studied on her. "Don't gotta look," he said, "but we might not can get her up 'less you help pull."

Lurlene eased closer to the edge, leaned out a bit, looked down. Retta figured to grab on if her legs give out, but Lurlene kept to it hard.

Was a bad sight down there, forty-foot drop, Cammie face-down on the gravel bar. She'd managed to drag herself a good ten feet toward that twist of shallow fast-water, smearing a trail of blood in the orange chert. Either hitting the rocks took some minutes to kill her, or she wound up going black and the cold got her. Woulda been no way on or off that bar, 'cept through that ice-cold water.

Already down there, TJ cut the corners off Cletus's old tent and spread the faded green canvas beside her. At barely fourteen and built skinny like a Daddy Long-legs, how that boy managed to climb down the icy bluff face without he should get busted up like that girl, well, it struck a wonder, it did.

Lurlene turned away, put arms against that tree, buried her face in sleeves, made sounds of the kinda hurt don't ever stop. Retta wished it hadn't ended this way, but she and Randall had been layin' wishes on that girl since the day it started, all the good it did her. You can't live in a world of wish.

TJ pushed his makeshift tarp against the dead woman, but he fumbled, hands shaking. He took a deep breath, studied the situation a minute, then got her by the shoulders and pulled her about halfway on and rolled her over. Cammie's face had busted to pieces, bits of rock bedded in the meat, that scar on the tip of her nose never to matter no more.

TJ turned away, then tuned up and started crying. Just stood there and cried, he did, like first time he'd had to figure what dead really means, like listening for Cammie singing in the woods from now on means hearing nothin' but the birds and a creek that runs no matter who comes and goes, like doing this *man's job* your 76-year-old great-uncle can't do still leaves you feeling too much like a little boy.

"TJ?" Randall called, unusual patience in his voice. "Now, you got to finish so you can get her covered up. Do right by her, son."

The boy wiped his face with a sleeve, then tugged at her feet until he got her full on. He straightened her out, thought better of it, and with some effort pulled her legs forward so she lay curled on her side. Pulling one end of the canvas over her, he gathered the corners and cinched them together, struggling to get her stiffened body to shape right. Satisfied, the boy sat right down on the cold gravel and worked hard at not crying some more, all the good it did him.

"Let's get this done," Lurlene said, catching Retta with a start. "New deputy'll be pokin' around soon; can't risk him figurin' out."

TJ settled himself down and went to work, tying off both ends, setting a loop and hooking it for lift. He turned over the bigger rocks that showed blood, then tossed the small ones into the creek before Daddy Long-legging his way back up the bluff rock. Randall tied the rope to a tree, and all four set to pulling up Cammie's body. Took 'em some work to get her up over the edge, but once they got off the bluff rock, it proved easy to slide her on the icy ground, straight to that unfenced plot where the earthly remains of kin rested, most of their markers long weathered away. Randall fetched a shovel from the truck and started a hole, but TJ did most of the digging, near done after forty-some minutes when he stopped to catch his breath.

Lurlene said, "As many times we found her looking down at that spot, she was thinking on doing this—doing this to herself."

"No!" TJ said, digging again, stabbing that shovel through layers of Tennessee chert. "She wanted—to get closer—tried to climb down is all. Slipped and fell." His eyes watered on him, nose all snotty. He handed the shovel up, jumped up and shimmied out, stood there and drawed himself up. "She figured this holler couldn't be, 'cept with her songs. No way she'd a-wanted to leave us without."

Maybe the boy said truth, or maybe just what needed heard. Either way, Lurlene would have to find some kinda way to live without her girl.

And now she had one more heartbreak to picture how it happened.

Lurlene stood there, face showing hurt with no place to put it, waiting while TJ and Randall managed to lower Cammie's body gently to its resting place. Retta wished a preacher could come, not that Lurlene and them believed anything, but just to have some kinda way to mark the passing. Girl never left the holler from six months on, never learned to talk, never got seen by a soul these past few years 'cept that dead deputy and the kinfolk gathered here now, three outta the four now more short to this world than long. Nobody could think a thing to say, which sure didn't seem right. Preacher would have sounded like something bigger than this holler cared about a dyin'.

So TJ started to sing.

No words, just one of them songs like Cammie always sung. Randall's eyes swole, got watery, and he put his hand on his heart. Lurlene tried to look calm, respectful, but she wound up bowing her head to cry. Retta couldn't see clear, eyes all leaky, no custom for her, but that hole in the ground . . . that pile of dirt. She had to look away, into the woods, all gleamy with ice . . .

Someone there.

A face, watching.

Frozen, caught.

The deputy? No, a woman, a stranger, seeing the whole story, clear as day, the holler's secret right out in the open, dug up and put back on the creek-bed gravel-bar for all to see.

Click.

Randall had leveled his rifle, cocked it.

TJ fell quiet, eased over to the pickup, lifted his shotgun from the bed, trained the business end on that woman.

She made like to ease her way backwards, all the good that would do her. TJ broke loose, rabbit-streaked beside the double-rut, flashed a ways behind her. She turned like to run, but willy-nillied on the ice, flour-sacked her backside to the ground, pulled herself back up one-handed. Randall eased toward her, TJ now thirty, forty yards behind.

"Stay here," Retta said, hand on Lurlene's arm. She shadowed Randall, unsnapping the pouch holding that fish-knife in her coat pocket.

Woman made like to run, couldn't get a foot to hold. She whirled one way, then the other, surrounded now. She picked up a stick, made like to swing it one-handed, fight all rised up in her . . .

But she had no chance, no choice, and her shoulders slumped, the fight gone as fast as it had come. This woman had fought before, and giving up had learned to come easier than losing. She sat right down on the snowy ice and put face to hands, shoulders all a-shake. TJ moved in, stopped at twenty feet, lowered his gun a bit, ready, careful. Boy knows to watch his aim when a group is climbing slippery rock, wading fast water, sliding shiny ice, or moving on a down animal from both sides. But what do you do with a soul don't care no more? Warn her away from the bluff drop?

Everybody stepped closer, both women now looking down at her. Woman looked up, her lip split wide open in two places, one eye black.

Maybe twenty-some, she held one arm close, like maybe broke or pulled out the socket. "Jus' kill me," she said, and she meant it. "I'm dead anyway. Least then he'll be left to wonder."

Lurlene knelt down, lifted her face up, pushed long streaks of dirty blond out the way. "Who done this to you?"

The woman jerked and twisted her head at the snap of a branch, then took a deep breath, closed her eyes.

TJ put his own eyes every direction, listened close. That boy could hear willowflies rising from the water, come early spring.

Lurlene said, "How'd you get here, hon?" Must be liking this girl, whatever reason, "hon" never coming easy nor often. Lurlene sat right down on the ice with her. TJ relaxed a bit, fidgeted with his gun.

Five full minutes, they waited, and when the girl looked, Lurlene just raised her eyebrows and waited some more.

"I come east," the woman said, "—from over the Arkansas line?" She went on, pausing 'tween bits, sometimes askin' instead of tellin', like she needed to be told it's right, or wondering if it's okay to say. "I finally put Leroy's sorry butt out, so he come back and burned my place, then beat on me for lettin' him do it."

"How come you to be *here?*" Randall said, suspicion before hospitality for the uninvited.

"Drove till my car made bad noise and started smokin'—pulled up the gravel road yonder? Tried to park for the night, hit a slick ice patch, slid right over the edge."

"Deep over there," TJ said, voice lower, tough-sounding, like a bear cub on its hind legs looking big. "Big drop—all growed over, too."

Randall gestured up toward the roadway, so Lurlene made like to help the woman up, but both wound up helping each other. Retta stood back, watched.

"How come you to hold that arm?" Lurlene asked as they started walking, Randall back a ways, TJ well out front.

"He stomped all over it when I fell," she said, a sniffle trying not to cry. She eased it out from the sleeve of that ratty wool, shivered from the cold, the man's undershirt no good, considering. All swole, dark and colored like a caught bluegill that's give up ever touching water again, even a scraped spot like a bass-tail at bed-fanning time. It didn't look so much broke as angry.

"Married to him?" Lurlene asked, gently helping her pull the coat back up, urging her on.

She shook her head.

"Won't give you up?"

"He'll be out to Jack's place for now—but soon as he comes off that drunk? He'll figure out can't expect me to come back—ain't no place to come back to—so he'll head out to see can't he find me. I got nobody, 'cept maybe a friend workin' remodels with me over to Castor's—when he can find us work?—but she lives with her mom and them, no room for me."

Retta said, "He won't be thinkin' past state lines, not with no direction to guess."

All three women helped each other up the chert piled alongside the double-rut, Randall and TJ still keeping their distance, weapons ready. They kept to the gravelly middle till they come to a gravel-scatter running into the deepest drop. Scrub, jack pine, quite a few discouraged spruce, and a patch of sycamore stealing most of the sun filled the space, no car in sight; but a powerful whiff of burn seemed to be sneaking around the misty cold, the smell of gas and oil. TJ walked down the road a piece to find a good spot, then worked his way down snag-to-scrub, disappeared in thick.

"Engine done burned!" he shouted with a boy-squeak from somewhere below, the mean low voice forgot. "Front tires melted, glass broke—nothin' but junk in the first place!"

"I been meanin' to bring a 'dozer through here," Randall said, "—flatten this part, push some into that drop-off. Might could cover the car right up, never know it's buried there."

The woman's eyes went big, and she stepped back, scared.

"No hurry," Retta said. "Can't see it 'less you're looking for it, and maybe not then."

Sounds of the car door opening come up from the scrub, all pig-squeals and clanks, then more squealing as it closed after a minute. The boy appeared where'd he gone down, oversized purse under his left arm, no telling what-all poking out of it. He presented it to the stranger. "That's all," he said, "'less something in the trunk."

She shook her head, then with that good arm clutched the bag to her chest, all she got left.

"Gettin' late," Randall said, and they all worked their way back to finish conducting a funeral, rifle and shotgun propped against a tree, woman's purse on the ground beside 'em.

TJ sang again, and the stranger even cried as they covered Cammie over. They stood back while TJ gathered branches and disguised the grave, scattering more close by to hide their work, give dirt time to settle 'fore anybody could notice. He eyed a gravelly patch off to the side where weeds never took a liking, no doubt worryin' someone might figure 'em out, then started to go after more branches, but Retta told him, "That's enough."

And that woman stood there watching every bit of it.

Randall looked to Retta, and she knew what he was thinking.

"We need to stop by Lurlene's quick-like," Retta said, all matter-of-fact, "so we can get home 'fore dark." They all headed through the woods, the stranger who'd seen their secret keeping to the middle of the group, nobody saying a word.

At Lurlene's place, TJ fed sticks into the kitchen pot-belly, then started adding splits to the parlor fireplace while Retta pulled one of Lurlene's vinyl chairs from the dining room and placed it middle of the tile floor. She gestured for the woman to sit, then gently took the purse from her. Randall stood to the side, holding his rifle. TJ kept working the fire up front.

Lurlene helped her out of her coat, clucked and shook her head at that arm again, offered the girl some water.

"Whiskey," Retta said. "Pour it big." She looked at Lurlene, and finally it seemed to dawn on her cousin what might be about to happen.

What *had* to happen.

The girl trembled a bit, but said nothing. She downed the glass in five swallows, set it on the floor. Didn't take long before she slumped some in the chair, head looser, eyes a bit glassed-over.

Finally, Retta spoke. "Got nobody but that man lookin' for you?"

She shook her head.

"Weren't figurin' to go back, was you?"

She snorted at the very thought. "Can't never go back. He knows ever'body in the county."

"No place else to go?"

"Got nothin' and nobody."

"And not a soul knows which way you come?"

She shook her head.

Retta put a hand in her coat pocket. "You said you hit a patch of ice, went off the road?"

The girl nodded, then closed her eyes.

Randall said, "Weren't no ice on that high part—all gravel."

TJ came into the room, the boy looking confused.

"Step out on the porch, son," Randall told him. "Wait for us, and don't come back in, no matter what you hear."

TJ's eyes went wide, then darted back and forth between the woman in the chair and his great-aunts, finally settling his gaze on Retta's hand in her pocket.

Randall raised his voice a bit. "I gotta tell you twice?"

TJ backed up, stood there a second, then turned and hurried out to the front porch, closing the door firmly behind him.

Retta said, "So you slid off the road where they wasn't no ice?"

Tears formed shiny smiles under the girl's closed eyelids, then broke loose and run south with a quickness. She looked sick now, hard time staying in that chair.

Retta demanded, "How come you to go off the road up there?"

"I could see dark over that side," she said quietly. "Deep . . . Soft . . ."

"Didn't figure to leave this holler ever again, did you?"

The woman tried to shake her head, but it lolled to the right, wouldn't come back up.

Retta said, "Figured to be dead by now."

The woman just sighed.

Retta moved fast.

The woman opened her eyes—

The knife flashed.

Weeks passed before the new deputy got around to pulling up front of Lurlene's place. He stepped out of his dusty Chevy Tahoe, put his eyes every which way quick-like. "Afternoon, ladies—young man."

"Deputy," Retta and Lurlene acknowledged, coming down from the porch. TJ paused from painting the porch-rail and nodded. Birds hollered from every direction, that ice storm forgot by now, early-spring nesting places a matter of vigorous discussion.

"Y'all are really fixin' this place up," he said, nodding approval. "I just introduced myself to Randall up by the road. He's sure workin' that 'dozer good for a man his age. *Real* nice work on this road. *Real* nice," he repeated, turning to survey the smooth drive-up and new circular turnaround. "Doin' some work inside, too, looks like. Oh, where's my manners? I'm Deputy Kistler, born and raised in Humphreys County, just come east for this job."

Retta stepped forward, introduced herself and cousin Lurlene. TJ put down his brush and moved closer, then reached out to shake the man's hand as his great-aunt introduced him.

Lurlene said, "And that's my granddaughter, Cammie." She gestured to the young chestnut-haired woman painting the windowsill, her back to them, oblivious. Sounded like she might be singing to herself, barely heard over that bird racket and the roar of Randall 'dozing the highway access.

"Yeah, I heard about her," the deputy said quietly. "Never been right, they say; never leaves this holler."

"So sad," said Retta.

"But she's doin' quite well," Lurlene added, "and we're even thinkin' next year or two lettin' her try livin' with kin up north."

"Well, good for her," he said. "Hope it works out." Quieter, he asked, "Fragment off a round caught her in the head? Something about the end of her nose shot up, too?"

Lurlene nodded, sadness in her eyes. "Cammie!" she called to the woman. "Cammie!"

The woman turned, looked sorta vacant, maybe aware some, maybe not. The end of her nose was tore up, tip missing, ugly scar to show for it.

"If you're headin' out," Lurlene said to the deputy, "could you drop me out at the mailbox, save me half a walk? I'm expecting something important."

Deputy tipped his hat to the others, held the door for Lurlene.

Retta watched them drive out, then turned and smiled at TJ and the young chestnut-haired woman with the funny nose.

Cammie came down from the porch to stand between them, then put her arm around the boy's shoulder. "Up north?" she said, chuckling. "Why, when I get my share next year?—ain't no telling *which* way I'll head."

"Settle in a *college* town," TJ suggested. "Then I might could stay with you when I go 'way in a few years."

She laughed, then gave him a hug with that hurt arm, now mostly healed, bruises about gone, doing good. "You got a deal," she said. "Now, let's finish this paint and get to work fixin' up that bathroom."

Retta watched the Tahoe's trail of rising dust meet up with the big cloud where Randall 'dozed gravel.

Cammie and TJ went to work, singing again, louder'n birds, filling the holler with Cammie's "words," that song only the two of 'em could understand.

Vapor-Girl

*Ah, uses a fantasy world as metaphor in an allegory, this one does.
We have been helping a 15-year-old girl in Iraq put together her
first book, its subject a fictionalized tale focusing acutely on how
"girls" are treated in her culture. I wrote "Vapor-Girl" before she
was born, yet somehow it seems like it could be about her. We
could use more Vapor-girls. We need more Vapor-girls.*

Carmon stepped from his modest tar-house into middling black night and gazed toward the rocky mountain-high ridge. Vari-colored swirls of rising lightning mist lit starless tar sky with shimmering flashes, magenta fingers twisting among tendrils of phosphorescent teal and turquoise and tangerine before dissolving into the ether of nothing.

The vapors would rise strong and true on this rare night when neither of two moons dared show a shiny face to warn the emboldened tingle-winds back into the chasm where they bide.

"And will you ride with me, this my last time?" called the distant voice of Tamoo-girl from the night.

Carmon struck fire to light the see-pod, its yellow glow erasing sky even as it revealed the glistening eyes of Tamoo approaching from her tar-house in the lower-land. She stopped several paces away, then stood her vapor-board on its tail and shook her head, that way she had of fluffing her gleaming pink tresses.

"Still you ask them, the silly questions while I mourn," he answered, already failing in his plan to make happy where happy can never again dwell. As an older adolescent orphaned by an earlier ground-shake, he had been allowed to keep his childhood home and so to live his life as a man. Tamoo had just lost her father, her only family, to the recent great ground-shake, and now with no man owning her she would be sold to another at tomorrow's Assembly, her fate already known, a life serving the sons of Motticot the Elder, three brainless men of brawn requiring her to bear babies she would never be allowed to love.

"I mourn, too," she said, "so will you ride with me in my grief?"

"I would ride always with you, Tamoo-girl," he said, turning to pick up his board lest she see his eyes water even as his throat hurt. He had been riding the vapors with Tamoo since they were young children, this despite the harsh behavior of boys who resented how Tamoo's father let her ride like a man, how he allowed her to behave so unlike a proper girl.

She stepped closer to the see-pod, and her eyes sparkled, her hair flaming that iridescent pink. She had defied the Council of Propers once again this night by donning the swatches of mottled blue Frick-beast hide she'd skinned after a defensive kill, her ensemble revealing more than even the most immodest of proper girls would ever dare.

Carmon blushed and looked away, sensing he had made her smile again, the way she used to delight in teasing him back when there seemed hope his father's water-crystal collection would someday prove sufficiently valuable to outbid wealthier elders only marginally interested in a girl so easily given to shameful behavior and scandalous opinions.

But that day would never come. Carmon had been tracking Frick-beast with older men when a great ground-shake came, and by the time he made his way home bandits had passed through, leaving his parents' lifeless bodies but scant else, the secreted water crystals found and stolen. Now Tamoo wanted to sell her own dead father's home and land, and thus give the proceeds to Carmon so he might bid for her, but the Council of Propers deemed this unacceptable. With no man to claim succession, Tamoo's house and land now belonged to the people, its disposition a matter for the next Assembly, these final days dwelling there an act of mercy so she might mourn properly.

Carmon had known she would expect to spend this last night with him riding the vapors, the rare promise of moonless dark and starless tar sky roiling the chasm's bowels until winds roared and careless riders died while the brave soared higher than dreams.

Again, he looked away, so she moved closer, reaching out to touch his hair, a sin for which watchful eyes could have her punished. Having never allowed herself to fear the Council's wrath, she always stood defiant no matter how she suffered at their hands, always delivering the same words when allowed her moment to express remorse: "My punishment," she declared, "—it is to live among you."

He extinguished the see-pod and followed her gaze toward the world-edge ridge. The vapors had already begun sweep-splashing rocky crags with misty light, flashes of red and blue lightning bolts probing tar sky.

A surge in the scintillas of glowing vapor-specks streaked by, so she lifted her vapor-board high and tested the air. A gust of misty light caught the board and held it aloft. She fastened the hand-hide around her board's lightning hook, then headed down the trail, pulling her flyer on its power leash. She paused just long enough to look back with her practiced mien of exasperation.

He fastened his own hand-hide, then floated his board into the air and hurried after her, knowing that even on this last night to ride she would leave him behind if he dared tarry another moment.

They arrived just before half-night to find the vapors roaring truer that Carmon had ever seen. A score of riders had arrived and begun steeling themselves for adventure, men and adolescent boys who dared brave the biggest waves, younger boys relegated to watching from ledges jutting over the chasm—not too close lest a bolt of lightning blacken their bodies and steal their souls, or the emboldened tingle-winds lift them from their perches and carry them boardless to tar sky's certain death.

"Tamoo-girl, she come teach us," said Carmon's hunting friend, joining the pair. "Teach us ride big vapor, better than any man."

"Tamoo, she make us proud," said another of the youngers approaching.

A third hurried up to the group, panting with excitement. "Kenta brothers, they say ride tandem this night. No way, I say. Nobody since grandfather's friends ride tandem, not die."

They all turned to watch, and Carmon noticed many harsh looks directed toward Tamoo, this girl who still dared ride vapor surely knowing Motticot would punish her severely after tomorrow's Assembly. Tamoo would never ride again after this night, all knew, not on this world, not in this life.

The Kenta brothers launched their boards, Wain the more experienced, his younger Glin only now grown close to full man height. They missed the next big bolt, so they tossed their lightning hooks several more times until catching a smaller one, the electric tug pulling them gently into vapor streams flowing up from the chasm, each brother positioning himself to ride the biggest waves.

They surfed back and forth, testing the vapors' persistence, rising higher with each pass, then cutting toward the ridge side-by-side, almost touching. Along the front edge of great drafts they skittered between bolts until gradually settling into a consistent flow that might last long enough to test their skills. Younger Glin handed his hook to Wain, then carefully stepped to the rear of his brother's board.

Suddenly it flipped, flinging them both into the roaring surge. Wain grabbed his board and regained his footing while managing to hold Glin's lightning hook, but the younger disappeared in the waves, a dark speck buffeted by eddies of light and tossed into misty geysers, sometimes dropped into holes only to rise in time to be tossed again.

Wain raced frantically, stomping into the surges on pass after pass, finally catching a draft alongside the younger, moving closer, closer, reaching frantically lest the next explosion rip them apart.

And Glin grabbed the tail of his own board, his lightning hook dancing dangerously free until a great blue bolt pulled it into a merciless whirl. He regained his footing, holding on, seeking his chance, then skating into the fallout and riding outflow back to the shelf. He crashed to the ground, gasping and weeping, his brother soon landing close by.

They hugged each other without regard for all that is proper, but nobody cared, the vapor riders being an improper bunch, if that can be possible in this time, in this world. The crowd whooped its approval, this Kenta failure still the best attempt most had ever seen, and nobody had died.

The legend of riding tandem would remain just that, a fancy, never a possibility, but a most impressive show in its attempt.

As Tamoo moved to the edge and removed the hand-hide from her lightning hook, Carmon remembered again the harsh truth of this last ride with his lifelong friend. The night was passing too fast, surges already greater than ever seen, no way to continue braving such power and danger until daylight ignites the vapor-flow fires and burns down the mists.

He readied his board and gave the signal. She caught a bolt, and he grabbed it, too, just in time, slipping in behind her for a gentle ride exploring myriad ledges lining the chasm from launch-flat to the lowland drops. He moved beside her and held place as she circled back to catch gusts of lift, making passes over the crowd, many of the riders now trying to launch their own boards, a few already crashing on this most powerful of tar-sky vapor nights.

As she skittered this way and that, teasing the drafts, he never left her side. This always impressed his friends, the way they appeared to float connected through the sky, just as birds fly and fish swim, each reacting instantly to magical signals that move them in concert.

In these moments, it seemed their souls mingled to become one.

They caught a big wave and rode into the heart of the roiling storm, their skin electric with vapor tingles, wind whipping all fluff from their hair, crooked lightning grins blinding them as each bolt's after-laugh bellowed in their ears. The infinite force beneath their feet drove them higher and higher until they soared across the heavens, even as twisting tornado holes snatched them into spiraling plummets so they might catch new bursts to ride higher still.

They surfed to exhaustion, that sheer power of the greatest vapor rise now battering them until they had no choice but to skate across to the world-edge ridge-side of the chasm and rest on a precarious ledge, their lightning hooks sheathed, electric gusts roaring skyward a mere arm's-length from their faces.

"We have to ride cross *now*," he shouted, cupping his hands around her ear, decorum and all that is proper no matter, not now, not ever again.

She shook her head, then moved closer and shouted, "I will not return."

His heart pounded, and he recalled the story about a despondent young man who rode the vapors until he disappeared into the outflow mists that spill over the world-edge ridge and disappear forever, no way back.

"No!" he shouted. "Tamoo, you will die!"

"Apart from you," she cried, "I will die here, so I go where the vapors take me, maybe to a world beyond the edge!"

"It is sin to speak of that," he warned, but what he wanted to say was that she must choose her own destiny, and there are no sins except against the heart.

"My father," she yelled, "he believed our peoples came from beyond, a too-proper clan afraid of the world, and the chasm opened to keep us here. Our ancestors, they ride the vapors to cross for trade, but ground-shakes made the chasm too deep, the vapors too strong, and now we never remember the way home."

"But you might be wrong!"

She touched his hair, then stroked it gently, and their faces brushed as if he might keep her, and gentle fingers swirled around them and tickled their skin.

She stood and unsheathed her lightning hook, then looked at him tenderly, her eyes glistening in the phosphorescent hues of teal and turquoise and tangerine. "Never will the Council let you keep me," she yelled, "so I must give myself to the vapors!" She tossed her hook into the swirls and mounted her board. One look back with water eyes, and she disappeared into the roaring mists.

"Wait!" he called, jumping behind her, catching the next bolt and chasing her skyward. He would give up his last chance to cross for home, knowing in his heart that scant moments they might ride together mattered more than any certain future riding alone without her.

The closer he drew, the faster she sailed, catching every burst to ride higher and higher. He nearly caught her again and again, but she would plunge into another hole and skitter sideways to catch the next wave even at its most dangerous crest. Still he pursued her, his heart pounding, destiny screaming in his ears.

She caught the world's-end bolt, the biggest burst of all, just as he surfed in beside her, and they climbed together until they soared higher than the mountains, higher than absent moons, higher than the blackest boundaries of all that dwells 'neath starless tar-sky night.

He felt the board crack beneath his feet, and as their eyes met, he saw the fear in hers. She looked toward his board just as it shattered, its shards scattered in consuming flame.

She reached out.

And he touched her, held her, stepped closer to her, and put his arms improperly around her waist even as he gained footing on her board to ride in tandem like no two had ever ridden before.

Their movements became one, even as their souls mingled to sail into whatever the fates would deliver childhood friends who love now as woman and man.

The next blast pushed them ever farther from home, and in the distance beyond the edge of the world he thought maybe he glimpsed a great city, but he could not be sure.

They submitted to the crashing overflow, propelled by sheer torrents flowing over the ridge and beyond, now surfing faster than bolts as they cascaded down a mountain river of pure lightfalls.

They might live forever, they might die in the next heartbeat, but Carmon and his beloved Tamoo-girl would always ride the magic vapors as one.

Band Call-out

Music and art are called "the humanities." Musicians get that, especially when it's all we have left. Art will out, even when the humanity can't. Another version of this, differently titled, appeared in an anthology from Joyce Carole Oates. Thanks to Benjamin Wagner for the photo. I think some among us want— need—to find harmony even amid the most extreme dissonance.

That banged-up old black tanker car got left behind.
It must have been sitting there for many years, maybe decades, passing time on a split of secondary sidetrack, no place else to go. Debris and weeds choked the rails, as thicker brush grew up through its wheels and broken coupler.

Fuse sat cross-legged on the weedy patch of wannabe lawn in *the big yard*, just inside the pea-gravel track edged by razor-wired electric fences. Oval-walking convicts occasionally disrupted his view of the old tanker, as did the creepy crawl of a lethally armed perimeter vehicle, its skin a shiny state blue. At least you know that climbing the fence is precisely what triggers the patrol's violent assault. Fuse's psycho bunkie and his dawgs would crack an unsuspecting head for no other reason than the rumors they started. Like so many others in the joint, they live for the fool-rule: act stupid, put your business on front street, get yourself popped, and save face by calling the nearest body a *rat*.

A daddy killdeer bird swooped in and challenged Fuse with a cautionary dive, then landed a dozen feet to the left and glared threats before relieving his mate at their ground nest marked by a bright orange traffic cone. *Don't step on the baby*, somebody had thought to alert the other prisoners, likely some nature lover who'd just as soon padlock a human skull and stab a body fifteen times before ghosting into the crowd.

The prim-looking killdeer fed its lone chick, then settled in to keep an eye on Fuse.

Beyond the nest, that line of counterclockwisers followed the oval's arc along the back fence, the backdrop a grassy berm blocking views of the new high-security joint next door.

A train clanked and squealed its way across the road, then down the spur track that ran alongside both prisons. Every day, the train delivered chemicals to a small paint factory on the other side. Fascinated by trains as a boy, Fuse liked to sit right there most afternoons—weather and emergency counts and clear-the-yard assaults permitting—to watch the replacement of yesterday's empty tanker with today's full one. The whole process always seemed out of place, this glimpse of purpose and productivity in a rusty, falling-down city, industrious men commanding monstrous and mighty machines.

Fuses's bunkie couldn't fathom the relationship between man and machine. Last night during one of his rages, he destroyed their cell fan. Apparently it had been disrespecting the over-inked lunk by intentionally rattling and wheezing to interrupt another twelve-hour sleep, his rest inexplicably essential for fueling a mind that never actually shifted out of idle.

His tantrums had been escalating since two slash-and-burn shakedowns in a row convinced him a snitch must have kited about the piece of steel he'd been bragging about. Hearing whispers of blame, Fuse had noticed several glares and hostile gestures.

Heavy Metal wandered over, set his guitar and battery-powered mini-amp in the weeds, then sat cross-legged and nodded with a *'Sup?* He got the Heavy Metal moniker for playing heavy-metal guitar—quite deftly—just as Fuse had picked up his own tag for favoring fusion style during his stint on keyboard in a mishmash cover band out at the regional prison. Wiry and muscle-bound, the long-haired metal-head claimed several names and aliases, just enough to confuse his incoming mail, though only the six digits on his door card truly mattered.

The engine passed them and grunted as the whole train clanged its way to a stop. The engineer climbed down and joined two men walking from the rear. He studied his clipboard and the numbers on a shiny white tanker, then headed back to the engine. The other two uncoupled the tanker at both its front and rear, then switched the rails to a third sidetrack heading over to the paint-factory pumps. The train grunted several more times as it backed in and picked up yesterday's empty tanker. It pulled it alongside the prison fence before backing into the full tanker. It coupled with a clank and hiss, then moved forward past the switch. It backed into the factory again, this time leaving the tanker before pulling out and backing up to couple with the rest of the train. Maybe fifteen minutes total, the engineer reversed the whole assemblage across the road and faded into the 'hood.

Still, that banged-up old black tanker car on the other track got left behind.

The show over, Metal dropped his news with a smirk. "Mo says your keyboard's out in the warehouse, and Doug's gonna let you have it, since they didn't catch on before putting in your order." The approved vendor had put a five-octave Casio with stand on sale for $79, only four bucks over the property-policy price-per-item limit; so he'd written them a letter proposing a $10 credit for withholding the otherwise contraband metal stand, and they wrote back agreeing to the $69 without it. That money order to his inmate account from Fuse's granny right before she died proved worth saving all this time. The business office started rejecting everybody else who tried to order a keyboard the same way because they discovered the official sale flyer only listed the $79 deal. All his years down, this marked the only chance for Fuse to order a board with adult-sized keys.

"You still playing with that butt-kisser up there?" Metal asked, referring to Mo.

Metal used to be up in the unit with Fuse and Maurice—"Mo" for *Modern Jazz*. Then a shakedown that turned up the program's "borrowed" effects pedal caught Metal a theft ticket and cost him his Saturday afternoon music-room slot. Then his tatt gun and makeshift soldering pencil sent him to the hole. When he got out, he landed over in the other building. Fuse had taken to sitting outside Mo's cell several evenings a week to play music with their earbuds joined by a homemade splitter. The big old black man, who looked like he'd waded into a few too many fights back in the day, more than knew how to dance his fat fingers up and down the neck of his knockoff Les Paul-style guitar.

"No, Slim won't let me use his toy anymore." Slim's two-octave *I'm a Rock Star!* mini-key by Hasbro or Mattel or Fisher-Price wasn't worth the frustration anyway.

"You put in for your own music slot?"

"Yeah—more than a year ago."

"The rappers who snaked *my* slot—Doug says he's gonna cut 'em loose. Two rode out anyway, and he's pissed about smelling weed and cock-sweat every time they've been in there."

"But I don't have a band."

"Put me on the callout with you. Grab Reggie to play drums. Get Mo on bass—at least till someone else rides in. As Doug's music clerk, Mo could help push for Fuse to get that slot."

"You *hate* Mo."

"Yeah, well, he's the best on the compound for now."

"But all you play is metal."

"Man, I'll play anything. I just want back in."

"All original—no covers?"

"Only," Metal said. He smirked as he unpacked his guitar and plugged in his effects and mini-amp. He would answer with his hands.

"So this is how you do your time, huh?"

Metal fine-tuned a couple of strings. "It's play music or fight. Oh, by the way—"

The killdeer craned his neck to hear.

"You need to watch your back. Your bitch-ass bunkie is still talkin' shit about you."

Even though Fuse used earbuds, Psycho threw tantrums every time he tried to work on music in the cell. The mere sound of fingers striking plastic keys upset that delicate equilibrium of fixations and obsessive compulsions. Every time the doors broke, Fuse and his Casio headed for base, or afternoons with Metal in the big yard, or evenings in the doorway to Mo's cell.

"Two more weeks," Mo said one night. "Tee-Bey got paper, so he'll be ridin' to Regional for prerelease. Ray-Ray and Westside'll make a play to keep the slot, but Doug says you been here longer. They gotta wait their turn."

Working with Mo opened new ways of approaching music for Fuse. Some thirty-odd years ago as a *fish*—a first-timer—Mo had fallen in with some old-head musicians who taught him the rudiments of old-school jazz guitar. Mo moved on to teach himself new styles by listening, experimenting, and playing with others who'd come and gone in the decade since. Mo offered Fuse some of his original material, meticulously charted, and taught him efficient ways to chart his own. They impressed each other, together shaping sounds that conjured exhilarating new realms beyond the fence, whether to make bold statements or simply discover whatever they might find. The progressions, the patterns, the styles—Fuse picked up many, then surprised Mo more than a few times by passing along some of his own. Still, what Fuse liked most was Mo's tendency to hold back rather than diving all in.

"Don't hit that flat five every time you run down a blues riff," Mo would lecture. "Save that and the flat six, even the major seventh or minor third. Use 'em only when the chords shift, and then only *maybe*. Make everybody ache for 'em, wonderin' when you'll let 'em slide *with* you."

Fuse brought several of Metal's songs to their two-man sessions, too, surprising Mo with how that *bool*shit metal could offer clever nuance and space to layer surprises, sometimes even a groove that jumped the rails and cut its own path toward whatever new places it might dare find.

One evening Mo was shuffling through his chart, looking for something to work on, when he caught Fuse craning to see the faded and creased photo of a young black woman tacked to his bulletin board, her arms in the air, apparently dancing. "That's my little girl—LaTisha," Mo said quietly. "She's thirty-four now."

Fuse nodded. "Very pretty." He had lots of questions. *You in touch? She live in The City? Ever come to see you? Grandkids?* Still, he knew you don't ask, not if you really do care. Mo would say only what he wanted to say.

"She was born after I got locked up. I've never seen her. Her and her mama wanted nothin' to do with me. Then her mama got cancer and couldn't beat it, so she sent me the picture toward the end, said maybe I deserved that much, see what I missed."

Fuse nodded and waited, resisting the urge to touch his keys.

Mo pulled his footlocker over, fumbled with the padlock, and dug through layers of paperwork. "You ever had any kids?"

Fuse took a deep breath, not sure how to answer. "A daughter," he said quietly. "Amanda—Amanda, with the beautiful smile."

"No contact now?"

Fuse shook his head.

"Her mama, neither?"

Fuse shook his head again. "Nobody out in the world since Granny died."

"That sucks." Mo located a tattered blue pocket pocket-folder. "Me, neither—not since Moms died." He pulled out two small sheaves of song charts, one set neatly handwritten, the other photocopied from the same material. "Doug made me copies," he explained, setting one sheet atop the footlocker, handing its companion to Fuse.

LaTisha's Dance, read the title.

And they played it—several times, several ways. Mo marveled at the nuance and style and layered rhythms Fuse added. Sometimes the big guy drifted into wistfulness, closing his eyes as he played, once turning away and wiping his face.

"She would like that," Fuse offered as Mo put the charts back into his footlocker.

"She'll never hear it," Mo replied, his frustration palpable. "I'm doing *all day*." Life without parole—a death sentence, he'd got . . . the slow way.

"I'm eligible in fourteen-some," Fuse said. "Maybe I can play it for her."

Mo looked surprised, then very serious. He pursued his lips and rubbed his beefy head. "Maybe."

The days leading up to the first callout on Fuse's new Saturday slot found him distracted. He worked on the first seven songs they'd selected—three of Mo's, two of his own, and two of Metal's—but often found himself also playing variations on the "LaTisha's Dance" theme. That invariably led to pondering an unwritten song of his own that he couldn't even begin to hear, no matter how deeply he listened for "Amanda's Smile."

Then his bunkie went to the hole after another shakedown, word on the yard being that he had some steel and somebody snitched. Rumors wafted back several times that Psycho's road-dawg, Jack, was telling people Fuse got him popped. That kind of talk might fade for lack of credibility, or escalate if more instigators jumped on board.

Sitting alone late one night in his cell, the bottom bunk now empty, Fuse set up the keyboard, plugged in earbuds, and began to play. He ran through all seven songs, but couldn't really remember actually playing them. He messed around with "LaTisha's Dance" a few times, but found himself distracted and frustrated. *Amanda* kept skittering just beyond his grasp, and for the first time in his entire *bit*, he realized that trying to connect with any part of his world lost beyond time or those fences inevitably left him feeling alone and afraid. He had nobody, no one to call, no one for mail, not a soul who cared whether he lived or died. With Psycho gone, he couldn't even busy his mind by hating.

The next day, he sat with Metal and Reggie in the yard, running through the same seven songs while storm clouds rolled in from the west, a gusty breeze blowing cold, the smell of rain stirring the paint fumes in the air. Short and stocky with a random splay of jet-black hair, Reggie mostly worked the patterns, trying beats by slapping his legs and scatting, his mouthed cymbal-swells spraying spit. They paused to watch the train take one and leave one, even as it ignored that beat-up old black tanker. The killdeer seemed unimpressed by it all, his priorities tending toward family.

"If we have time," Fuse said, "I'd like to try a Mo song about his daughter—real personal."

Metal shrugged, honoring his promise to play *anything*. He'd proven amazingly adept at exploring other genres and styles, no doubt proud of his prowess, though loath to admit he actually reveled in material he considered beneath head-banging and metal shredding.

They ran through Mo's song a few times, and Metal clearly understood what it meant, what it *could* mean. He found poetry in the images it conjured, grace in the notes, the tentative reluctance of a shy young woman yielding to her own rhythms, the yearning for a father she never met, the longing of a damaged man whose melody can't be constrained by the razor-wired electric fences.

At some point, two young black guys walked up to them, pants hanging low, dark scowls highlighted by narrowed eyes. "You on the music callout now?" one demanded.

"We *all* are," Metal said, setting his guitar in its case.

"That's 'posed to be ours," the other insisted.

"That's on Doug," Metal said.

Reggie tilted his head toward Fuse. "*He's* been on the list a year."

They glared for a moment as the killdeer watched warily.

"We'll see," one said. They turned and walked away.

Reggie snorted his derision. "They wanna start somethin', *I'll* start somethin'."

"They'll try anything to get that slot back," Metal said. "We might need to take a few people and have a talk."

Reggie added, "With Jack, too. He's still on that bullshit about Fuse. It's about time to tune *his* ass up."

"He's in my unit," Metal said. "I'll tell him shut his fuckin' mouth— or we got a problem."

Big drops of rain splattered their instruments. Everybody scrambled to pack up.

Lightning flashed in the distance.

"*Attention!*" called the loudspeakers. "*All yards are closed!*"

Never having been to the music space, Fuse followed Mo to the far end of the rec area, through the breezeway with an open-entry bathroom off to the right, then into the gym where incomers streamed in to grab basketballs and argue about the game that hadn't even started. A pair of doors in the far corner revealed a large storage area converted to a music room, Metal and Reggie already setting up. Two keyboards way better than the toy Fuse owned, real trap-set drums, amps, guitars, a bass for Mo to cut loose, more effects than Metal could channel on a hundred songs—all this had been waiting for them right here, so close and finally no longer out of reach.

So they played.

Fuse raced to learn all the keyboard programming. Metal tested effects to augment his new styles. Reggie tuned the drum-heads and rearranged the toms until he'd placed them just right. Mo bobbed his head, sheer excitement pumping the big old guy. They laughed, got serious, honed the precision of their charts, and drifted through improvs that took them places from which they returned only reluctantly. Fuse embraced the idea of holding back, leaving holes, saving those drop-ins and blues flourishes and major-seventh jazz highlights for only when they desperately needed expressing.

And Fuse finally knew this was how he could do his time. Four-teen-some years—more if the parole board didn't want to let him go—a personal keyboard right in his cell, real musicians gathering each week to listen to each other and sound back, a group of like-minders creating places and spaces where no outsiders could dictate what he dared feel.

When Reggie left to take a leak, Fuse started playing "LaTisha's Dance."

Mo went wide-eyed. He opened his mouth, but found no words as Metal quickly joined in on guitar, his chords and gentle slides first shimmering, then syncopating with delicate harmonics. Reggie came back and tried a simple rhythm. Mo shook his head and hit some bass-note beats, a catchy pattern, nodding toward the snare, the cymbals, guiding his percussionist. Reggie picked it up, embellishing with a wood block, a tom-tom backbeat. Mo added a swaying melodic bass line and quickly danced his way into the groove.

They glided through the song three times, each pass more expansive, more nuanced—more playful, yet ponderous. Fuse felt a twinge of melancholy, so he dared let it ripple through his fingers. That was for Mo, and Mo understood, appreciation in his eyes. This song called out to LaTisha, and though she never knew her father, they all knew him, now more than ever, and maybe the best his little girl could ever hope would be that others might tell her about him, with words or not.

Time eventually ran out, and Reggie bolted to meet someone on the walk. As a music clerk, Mo needed to stay behind to inventory the miscellany. Fuse and Metal headed out with their instruments, following gym stragglers through the breezeway.

Metal stopped to hit the urinal, so Fuse set his keyboard by the sink and grabbed a paper towel to wipe his sweaty brow—

Bam! Bam!

The side—of his head—

He spun and fell hard, skull slamming into ceramic tile. He reached with his hand, warm blood running through his fingers. He tied to glimpse what was happening.

Feet, several feet, the keyboard picked up—

Bam!

Back of his head, spreading toward the front, his brain screaming. He tied to raise up, but couldn't stop the spinning.

Blood all on the floor.

Metal slumped beside the urinal, eyes vacant, arm twitching, shirt drenched red, neck bleeding, hand bleeding, stabs, slashes—

Fuse laid his head in the puddle and drifted.

Man, it hurts.

LaTisha danced through the tableau, paused to look, then danced away; and Fuse looked for Amanda, her golden curls, those big blue eyes, sweet dimples, the smile of his adorable little four-year-old . . . For an instant he could hear her, but it got hot, too hot, flames roaring, smoke choking him, stealing his breath, smashing him with dark regrets.

You tweakin' that shit again?! screamed his wife, bursting in through the front door. *You're supposed to watch her—not get high!*

But the flames, the smoke—and she kept screaming even as he found her and dragged her outside. Flashing lights raced her to the hospital, her hands and arms burnt from trying but failing to reach their little girl. Handcuffs, county jail, court appearances where nobody comes, and finally word that his death-do-us-part wife couldn't figure any possible way to go on living without sweet little Amanda, so she gave up trying.

Please, Amanda, smile for me one more time . . .

"Dammit!" Mo bellowed, his voice echoing. "Oh shit—hold on."

Officers appeared, then stood around, waiting for healthcare staff to complete the paperwork that lets an ambulance into the compound. Hey, good luck. Fucking convicts.

"He's gonna need state shoes to ride."

Too much smoke, too much heat.

Hospital now. "What—what happened to Metal?"

"Who?"

"Man, it hurts."

"Sure it does."

Eighteen days in the segregation unit, and the swelling subsided, gashes closed, stitches grew out. His ear would never look right, and he couldn't quiet that incessant squeal on the left side, constant noise, worse when he buried his head in the scratchy blanket.

The door buzzed open. Office Silvestri pushed a cart holding his big green duffel into the room. The matronly black woman always looked after her guys and seemed to take it personally when something happened that wasn't called for. "Ridin' you out tomorrow, sweetie. Need to fill out the property slip."

No keyboard, no cheap-ass Chinese television, no gym shoes— just a bag full of state issue, Granny's final letters, and paperwork—too much paperwork . . .

"What happened to Metal?" he asked her.

She leaned close, sharing a secret, a breech of security. "He's still listed OTH," she said. "That's good; when they packed his property, they were told he wasn't expected to make it."

OTH—Out to Hospital.

Fuse didn't sleep much that night. He hadn't slept much at all since it happened. Head hurt too much, heat still too much to bear.

The next afternoon, he stood near the back exit of the healthcare office while they belly-chained and cuffed him. Some prisoner barely out of his teens came in from another joint, belly chain and cuffs. Fuse took the youngster's place in the transport van, *one out, one in*, then closed his eyes while they loaded property in the back.

"Run those boxes back to Regional," someone said, so instead of taking the main road, they used a cut-through along the railroad tracks. The driver stopped and rolled down his window to spend too long chatting with an officer patrolling the perimeter. The train crossed the road and pulled alongside them, Fuse's only close-up, his last chance to watch the daily ritual, *take one, leave one*.

Maybe Fuse would eventually find Metal out in the world—even Reggie, too. They might very well rediscover the places they'd conjured together that one time in a converted storage room of the prison gym when fences briefly stopped mattering. Probably not, though *What Could Have Been* is many a prisoner's only song.

But he would never see Mo again.

He would never be allowed to visit him, certainly never have a chance to play music with him. Fuse's instrument had disappeared, but at least Mo made sure his charts got packed. Good lookin' out.

Something got added, too, for there in the duffel bag patiently waited a tattered blue folder, photocopies of a natural lifer's most personal songs, the page on top titled "Latisha's Dance."

Fuse hoped someday to locate Mo's daughter, and he would never stop trying to remember Amanda's smile.

The train's mission complete, it crossed the road and faded into the neighborhood.

As the van pulled away, Fuse turned for one last look, just to be sure.

Again, that old banged-up black tanker car got left behind.

Ready for Company

The luckier among us get to feel like their world is in order, their people safe. For the rest, too often it seems the more we strive for order, the greater the disarray. Margie is not so much an exaggeration as I would like to think.

This place looks a filthy mess, Margie thought.

"Three miserable years," Babs announced, tromping around the kitchen, bagel in one hand, crumbs everywhere, juice dribble dribbling down the carton. "Three years today." She stabbed the calendar with a butter knife, then tossed it carelessly into the sink, greasy smudges and smears staining the stainless-steel basin. "That's three years more than *anybody* should try to live with the likes of you. I'm gonna mark the occasion by spending it the hell away from here." She bit the bagel, then wiped her hand on a dish towel as dribs and drabs of melting butter collected on the shiny tiled floor.

"Why don't you see how much *more* mess you can make?" sniped Margie.

"Is that a challenge?" Babs took another bite, then licked her fingers.

Widowed sisters in their seventies, they had agreed to split the costs and upkeep of sharing Margie's house. Babs had since squandered most of the proceeds from selling her own place, most on "loans" to help support her barely employed sons, not to mention covering the expenses generated by two never-married granddaughters whose sole talent seemed to be bearing babies by men who don't stick around. Margie never had any children of her own, nor did she envy deluded women who pretend to find joy in constantly picking up after ill-mannered, unkempt brats.

Babs nibbled the bagel's crust, then tossed the whole mess into the wastebasket, a dollop of butter now splotching the receptacle's polished lid.

Margie noted all the damage, then followed her sister out of the kitchen. "You're going to Irma's," she said, more statement than question. An older shut-in with her own apartment across town, Irma would ask Babs to take her shopping, then monopolize her for the rest of a day, the two of them sprawled on couches watching soaps and eating fried bologna sandwiches. Margie had tried going along once, but the filth and stench in that place made her ill, mess everywhere, grime and mold and bottleflies all indifferent to the very notion that any self-respecting occupant would ensure that such encroachers find themselves most assuredly unwelcome. If Irma really wanted civilized company, she would have to scour that place top to bottom, then air it out a few days and scour it again. Until then, she must necessarily settle for Babs, the one who from the time she learned to walk never seemed even to notice any kind of mess, let alone care enough to do something about it.

"Stay out of my room," Babs said, pausing in front of Margie's decorative hallway mirror. She pulled a comb through her hair before adding an unnecessary finger-swipe of lipstick from the compact in her ragged bag-lady tote. Margie could spend hours in front of a mirror and never look as good as Babs would blowing in from a windy rainstorm. Long ago teenage boys had seen it, as had the men they became, and Margie always envied Babs that. But then Margie had met her own Harold, and he appreciated a woman who takes pride in how she inhabits her world, a home that outwardly reflects her inner character, revealing more than what a mirror finds in a hurried face.

"I have no interest in your room," Margie said. "I try to avoid that pigsty."

"No," Babs countered, pulling on that threadbare coat that hadn't seen a dry-cleaner in years, "you fight the urge long as you can, then barge in and set to cleaning until no self-respecting pig could live there anymore." She grabbed her purse and stormed out to that old Lincoln of hers in the driveway, then drove off in a cloud of blue smoke. She would no more think to run that rattle of claptrap through a carwash on the way home than she would to park it in the garage where it belonged, a reasonable request Margie had broached umpteen times, her efforts no more effective than talking to the wall.

Margie wiped the juice carton, then placed it spout-out in the refrigerator's neatly arranged row of drink containers, second shelf, left. She cleaned up the crumbs, washed the butter knife, wiped down the sink, and mopped the floor, then noticed the tile looked scuffed, so she stripped and rewaxed it, not satisfied until it positively glowed. She looked forward to these days when Babs would go to Irma's, each affording a rare chance for Margie to put everything in order without somebody coming right behind to make a new mess.

She scrubbed all the appliances, cleaned the toaster tray, and decided to take down the light fixtures to wipe out dust. She disposed of a repulsive dead fly that had escaped her notice by cleverly lying in the shadow of the bulb-socket's hook. Babs could turn lights on and off from now until the end of time and never notice the dirt and debris building up, not unless it got so thick no light would pass. Even then, she would probably just buy a new lamp, no doubt at some yard sale on the seedy side of town. "What?" Babs would say when Margie pointed out the mess. "—you expecting company? Only ones ever come here is *my* young'ns, and they'd just as soon *not* have to spend a minute more than necessary in this sterile, slip-covered monument to cleanser."

Oblong patches of window light patterned the floor, showing window-glass streaks wrought by an overnight spattering of rain, so Margie mixed her own formula of glass polish, store-bought spray-bottle standards having proven inadequate for the task. The air fresheners needed replacing, too, manufacturer's claims of long-term protection from infiltrating odors often falling short after mere weeks. She chose lilac, then paused for several breaths of fragrance before unleashing her sturdy vacuum cleaner on the hallway rug, twice this way, twice that, then once around again, the critical final lap being what most people never realize catches that last ten percent of whatever's been roused but not yet caught. She switched it off, studied the result, then closed her eyes and listened.

Peace and quiet.

No raucous cacophony of game shows ding-ding-buzzing from the TV in Babs's room. Lilac was starting to nudge the lingering scents of pine and lemon and precisely diluted vinegar and ammonia.

She pictured the house, its tasteful accents embellishing functional lines, soft doilies floating atop polished granite surfaces, porcelain-bowl waters offering assurances in precise hues of antiseptic blue, carpets still as pristine as new swatches in the flooring store's giant binder of interior-landscape dreams.

Still, something felt out of place, not quite right, like a burn in the cushion, some stain on the rug, those spots of spit-up on a toddler's hand-sewn heirloom dress. Babs's room stood before her, and without opening her eyes Margie sensed a dirty plate behind the door, half-drunk bottles of soda, crumbs scattered on soiled linen, dust deep enough to write one's name in, and beyond that a festering gas-station of a bathroom that would turn even a hobo's hardened stomach.

Margie shook her head, then spread newspapers to change the vacuum cleaner's bag before putting it away, its cord neatly coiled inside the trap-door slot. She made herself a sandwich and coffee, then tried to read a magazine, but the very idea of Babs's room distracted her. It didn't feel so much that way when Babs was actually in there, mess strewn around the messer somehow at least somewhat more legitimate until it's left behind. Babs would be angry if Margie so much as went in there, let alone straightened up, but Babs liked to find any excuse to be mad at her sister anyway, so she might as well give her a reason.

Even worse than expected, the room looked like a hurricane had blown through, then summoned a tornado to complete the demolition. Dishes, clothing, food, bedding, books and magazines—and Babs had been trying to paint still-lifes again, leaving a disarray of bottles caked with paint, brushes thrust into a dirty glass of muddy water, spattered trays, soiled rags, canvas remnants, stretcher staples popped every which way, many trod into the carpet. Margie spent two hours cleaning before even tackling the painter's mess. Another twenty minutes—twenty more than Babs would have devoted to the task—and Margie had reduced it to an organized collection. Near-empty jars found their way into the trash, as did quite a few more she poured into others where colors matched. Once-frayed brushes boasted neat new trims, sparkling water soaked pristine sponges in a shiny new glass, and the injured carpet rested comfortably after a thorough nit-picking had eradicated its infestation of parasitic staples. Margie even cut new rags from an old table cloth, then arranged clean hand towels every place a wannabe artist might reach.

Another hour in the bathroom, tub and tiles scrubbed, mirrors shined, air redolent of springtime lilacs, and a real human being could finally stomach stepping in there again. Not having the time to do it right, Margie had at least brought Babs's space up to the level of tolerable.

"You can't combine colors when they're *different mediums!*" Babs bellowed, home before dinnertime for a change. She stomped around her bedroom like an agitated bull, messing up everything, even pulling the fresh sheets off her bed. "You *ruined* my paints! Why can't you—" She stopped for a breath, then literally growled. "You're not right in the head."

Margie refused to listen to any more of this abuse, this complete lack of gratitude. She retreated to the living room, every detail there, at least, just as she'd left it. She peered into the kitchen, relieved to find all still perfect.

Still down the hall, Babs was slamming drawers and closet doors, but then she fell quiet for a minute before charging out, suitcase in hand. She pulled on her ratty coat, announcing, "I'll not sleep another night in this house." Out she flew, skid marks marring the driveway, blue smoke spreading across the yard, haze lingering in the dusky light.

Fine, then.

Let her share that filthy rat's nest of Irma's. Margie had cleaned up after her little sister when they were kids, and she had cleaned up after her for the past three years. Now she would clean up after her once again, and that would be the last time.

And clean, she did, noticing how much easier it is when everything's so dirty that filth is easy to see, no stepping back to catch the right light or peering closer to find what lurks at the fringes.

She cleaned until the kitchen clock chimed midnight. Babs's room had improved immeasurably, despite her clutter still taking up space. Margie wanted to pack it all, stack it neatly in the corner, then call Babs's boys to drive three hours and pick it up, a clean slate before a new day dawns. That option not really feasible, though, Margie settled instead for concealing it as much as hiding places permitted.

She slept soundly, then rose and made herself breakfast, cleaning up as she worked. She read a magazine, watched a hello-morning show, then found herself down the hall peeking into Babs's room, trying to imagine turning it into a sewing room or maybe a showcase for her collection of figurines, but the more she tried to picture it, the more she knew Babs would inevitably return. Soon paints would be strewn here and there, linens rumpled, laundry on the floor, dishes and crumbs scattered about. As a girl, Margie could never free herself of little Babs, the pretty sister, the one everybody adored, the one Margie had been expected to bathe and dress and make presentable for company.

Babs hadn't returned by lunchtime, so Margie called Irma's to demand that Babs come take her things—"Oh, you want to come back?" she would say. "Well, I'm not sure . . ."

"Not here," Irma said, her voice still mouse-squeaky since the chemo a few years back. "She left yesterday, 'bout four o'clock, I'd guess."

"She didn't come back last night?"

"No, and I been here," she said, as if she ever went anywhere that Babs didn't take her.

Annoyed Babs would dare to worry her like this, Margie called her sister's oldest, Ricky, apparently waking him in time to get busy being unemployed until his afternoon nap. A second call to younger son Tony confirmed that neither of Babs's sons had seen or heard from her. Margie promised to contact them after making more calls. Problem was, she couldn't think of anyone else to try.

A car pulled into the driveway. Babs would get an earful about worrying everybody like that, but it proved to be a patrol car, two burly officers in rumpled uniforms coming to track dirt into the house, one taking a chair while the other flopped onto the couch, throw pillows scattered helter skelter. One held Babs's driver's license, the other a notepad, both taking turns talking, quiet, sympathetic, concerned. One said something about the apartments where Irma lived, the parking lot, engine still running.

"Found her slumped on the floorboard," one said.

"Appears to be natural causes."

Beautiful Babs, her lifeless face pressed into the grime and clutter of that rat's nest car. Babs, the pretty one, a china doll toddling around the room, big sister Margie dressing her like a princess only to find her minutes later with mess spilled down the front. Babs, sneaking up on her big sister with wet kisses, her sweet mouth all chocolate and marmalade and peanut butter. Babs, the looker, the lovely gal who didn't care any more about her own appearance than she did the places she inhabited. Margie never looked that good, no matter how hard she tried, the one thing always inevitably beyond her control.

The officer held something out, but Margie's eyes welled with tears, one neat droplet spattering the arm of her chair. She tried to listen, but nothing they might say now could ever put Margie's world back in order.

"Will you be okay, ma'am?"

The other offered his card, then settled for placing it on the table, atop the doily, out of place, crooked, its corner bent, the color all wrong. "Is there someone we can call?"

She tried to think, but suddenly the phone rang, and she couldn't talk, so the officer explained to Ricky that his mother had passed.

And the officers left quietly, leaving Margie all alone before she could think to ask them to take the paints, the canvas, the neatly trimmed brushes.

She wiped her eyes and stood, lost in a place now unfamiliar, so she tried to straighten those throw pillows, but she couldn't get them quite right, just as it had taken her years after losing Harold, the way that man liked to put his feet up and knock the pillows every which way, exasperating her until the day he died and took his messes with him.

Ricky called, his family packing for the trip, three or maybe four hours away—and Tony's, too, all coming the way people come when the worst happens, a houseful of nephews and their young'ns and their sloppy babies all converging on Margie's home.

Company meant fresh towels, new soaps, the linen changed.

Only three hours, four tops, but the officers had tracked dirt all over the carpet, barely enough time to get ready.

Margie hurried to the storage closet and retrieved her rug scrubber, supplies, cleansers. She set it up in the living room, there where Harold used to scatter the pillows, where Babs used to flick crumbs and watch soaps. Morning light cut through the window, backlighting motes dancing in the air, fresh dust coating the end tables.

She felt sick, so she closed her eyes and pictured how it all should look, how Margie would look at the funeral, how Babs even laid out would still look more beautiful than her big sister. Nothing looked right. Nothing would ever look right. Nothing ever had.

She opened her eyes and peered about. So much work lay ahead, she couldn't imagine where to start.

Company was coming, and the place looked a filthy mess.

Krab Kaper

These characters were introduced in my media-thriller novel Fantasy Patch. *Well, Flynn Durbett harkens back to my military-scifi-thriller* Invigilator. *I wrote this short piece to use during a promotional tour for* Patch. *I don't carry characters over from one tale to another, and these are the only exceptions except for my* Rich Mr. Fixx *series—so far. Still, I liked spending some extra time with these people. Dante's angles tend to be right.*

Some lettuce just leaves a bad taste.

I don't know why, but this critter won't eat the stuff, instead preferring collards and other greens.

So imagine warm light, cool breeze, a splash of gurgling water, eight explorable square feet, one climbing ladder of latticed sticks, a

thatch of tasty greens beckoning from above, and our hero methodi-
cally clawing his way upward for all he's worth—which is normally
about five bucks, free if you simply pick him up, as Taj did.

It's a hermit crab, about the size of a jawbreaker, the landlubber version found in tropical beach-side brush. This crab and its three crabby
cohorts hail from Gulfcoast Florida, having hitched back to Chicago
in a sack of shells collected by the four-year-old son of my youngest
producer. I normally frown on taking souvenirs from sites above water
and below, these being nature's mobile homes for myriad denizens wet
or dry, but young Taj didn't know better, so no major harm.

I help him and three other kids, all now dedicated hermit-crab
owners, as they outfit a large terrarium in the day-care area of our
video-production facility. Dabbing quick-clean non-toxic paint, each
decorates his crab's shell for easy identification, this despite my warning that these critters often change houses for better fit and to run-
way-strut the latest in chic crab style.

We provide a small plate of corn meal, little-bit fruit bites, and
other crabby snacks; but for some reason the one now climbing after
the greens always decides to pass when it's offered mere iceberg.

Apparently, some lettuce just leaves a bad taste.

So we're watching the crabs one day when my friend/client Flynn
Durbett stops by with a sackful of test products designed for kid
safety and/or fun learning. Flynn's the soldier-of-fortune character
first introduced in Stephen Geez's novel *Invigilator*, way back before
he settled down a bit and founded a company dedicated to helping
people protect themselves from a dangerous world. He needs some
marketing hooks, packaging, design—anything I might contribute as
his agency-of-record creative director. My name is Danté Roenik, but
Flynn's been occasionally calling me "The Image Maker"—ever since I
deigned to narrate Stephen Geez's novel *Fantasy Patch*, the tale of my
infamous tilting at pharmaceutical-conglomerate windmills. Yikes!
Turns out windmills are quite willing to shred anybody who dares get
in their way.

Flynn shows me a sort of child's poncho boasting swirls of fabric stitched to hold pocketfuls of kid-stuff—tearaways for safety, elastic gathers to avoid strangle-strings—all topped by a nifty hood with sewn-in sweatband crafted such that side panels pull away to ensure full peripheral vision when young street-crossing bike-riding skateboarders turn their heads to look both ways. Flynn has inked a distribution deal with a chain of big-box stores, a test-market roll-out in the Chicago 'burbs, but the product needs a name, a hook, and some cool images laser-screened on the front and back.

Big-eyed Taj dons the smallest in Flynn's Santa-sack, and I'm instantly reminded of a hermit crab, the swirling shell, this spiky-haired lad peering out from under the hood, his expression that sneaky escapade-plotting look of appraisal often found on little kids and littler crabs.

I notice the real crab has reached his goal, now perched atop the ladder, contentedly munching his greens as I paint an art-deco shell design onto one of Flynn's pullovers. The kids all want them, but each prefers to paint his or her own design.

And there's Flynn's hook: *KrabbShells*, pre-screened as a plain hermit shell, each including a small set of disposable fabric markers so pint-sized fashion plates can customize unique looks—or visit Flynn's company website for ideas and templates, a safe place to share photos of their own and to admire the works of other young artists.

Next we paw through Flynn's collection of new products. I'm intrigued by a tiny ball with a slot that reveals a mini-light and magnifying glass with tiny tweezer and gripper. They prove especially handy for examining real crabs up close and personal. We all want one.

Flynn trundles off to meet with the big-boxers. They're lucky to be working with such a good man who values loyalty and integrity, one who looks out for others and the world we share—unless you cross him or try to hurt a friend, but that's a longer story, actually two, both attractively priced in print or multiple ebook formats.

So *KrabbShells* sales rapidly climb that ladder for the big-box stores, and Flynn's company feeds on the green, but we're not in control of the promotion, and Flynn's contract doesn't confer veto power over the unacceptable: our retailer starts offering one free hermit crab with every *KrabbShells* sale.

I do encourage responsible pet ownership for young people to learn about caring for others. Hermit crabs aren't endangered, and they're certainly not dangerous, but I have a pet-store-chain client who rightly rails against such indiscriminate pet-mongering. Buy a hermit from one of her outlets and you're not getting out the door without the proper habitat, supplies, how-to pamphlet, and a thorough conversation. Living creatures are not toy prizes; they should be entrusted only to those who truly want them and will properly care for them.

The big-box buyers dismiss Flynn's objections, opting instead to enforce their contract in lieu of maintaining good faith between retailer and supplier. We're all angry about this, including the kids and their chums, most of whom want to voice their outrage. After some serious hand-wringing over where to draw the line between exploiting young'ns and nurturing their burgeoning need to self-express, I do what people so often pay me a lot of green to do: I orchestrate one bodacious media spectacle, nationwide coverage, a public-relations cesspool to mire the mid-city big-box headquarters of these crass exploiters of innocent crabs.

So picture this: more than two-dozen subtly supervised teenies and tweenies dressed as hermit crabs, their hand-painted *KrabbShells* emblazoned with "Kidz for Krabs," a crusading cadre marching sideways in the cutest camera-calling crabwalk you could ever imagine. These irate squeaky-voiced orators are delivering little-bit sound bites for sympathetically amused on-the-scene TV reporters, crowds gathering to gawk and chant, our urban beach awash in a growing tidal wave of righteous indignation.

In a surprising move, egregiously unprofitable for successful builders of bigger boxes, our adversaries opt out rather than address the problem, apparently preferring to retreat into their shells to avoid fostering an image of cavers-in to special-interest pressure.

So Flynn gets his product back, then re-launches with a smaller big-box that's been angling to out-box the bigger big-boxers. Cranking up the Danté publicity machine proves a cakewalk—a crabwalk, as it were—after the impromptu kid-protest already raised awareness about the irresponsible, um, spreading of crabs.

Besides, offering free *KrabbShell* handhelds that open to reveal a tiny light, magnifier, and tweezer/gripper crab pincers starts piling some serious green on Flynn's plate.

Taj's crustaceous little friend promptly moves himself into a bigger, more stylish shell, and the young'ns all learn about making planet-friendly choices when their own careers someday find them climbing that ladder in the age-old quest for a little bit of green.

It's a lesson fit for a sound-bite:

Some lettuce just leaves a bad taste.

Blind Is Love

I wrote this from several topic-prompts for reading to our writer's group at the city library (shout out to Librarian Laney!). I never published it anywhere. I kinda sorta forgot about it, but I like how it fits into this collection. When something hurts too much to see, is it ever possible not to look?

Ernest P. Wittling followed his practiced routine in preparing for Mary's daily three o'clock visit. He had served her sugar-sprinkled star cookies and coffee that first occasion some thirty-three years ago when she'd come talking about some sort of census or survey. He'd served her the same snack every day since.

After that first year he summoned the courage to profess his love, but she demurred for another year before succumbing to his wiles. Still, they agreed their affection ought remain best expressed only through daily visits with sugar-sprinkled star cookies and coffee.

Unfortunately, this day he failed to maintain the odd routine he had developed. He did correctly keep his eyes closed when he went to the front door to admit her, looking again only after the chaste love-birds briefly touched hands and turned toward the sitting room where he'd already meticulously laid out the sugar-sprinkled star cookies and placed the pot of freshly brewed coffee. He had correctly met expectations by briefly telling her about his day, dropping hints of his hopes and dreams, thus fulfilling his deepest need, that of knowing some-one cared about what happens in the cloistered world of an aging man otherwise loath to leave the comfortably safe surroundings of his long-dead mother's home.

"Tell me about your day," he urged, listening intently, apprecia-tive both that she cared enough to share, and proud that he respected the need for another lonesome soul to have someone simply listen. It mattered not that the details she shared had scarcely changed in the decades since that first serendipitous meeting. He loved her, and he loved whatever she had to say.

This day, as usual, she hardly touched her sugar-sprinkled star cookies, so he wrapped them for her, but she forgot to take them, as she did every day, and he placed them in the kitchen for tomorrow, as he did every day. Where he erred in his routine this time, though, occurred while letting her out the front door. Normally scrupulous about keeping his eyes closed as he bid her goodbye, this time as she reached the street to cross, a loud noise on the walkway startled him—and he looked.

He looked.

Looking allowed him to hear, and what he heard terrified him, that roaring engine, the squeal of tires, the awful—that—that *thump*, and that's when he saw it *because* he had looked, that Chevrolet, dark blue, lots of chrome, skidding right there in front of his eyes, with Sweet Mary's broken body crashed partway through its windshield, blood on the hood, the front quarter-panel smashed, and more blood.

Mary's blood.

He'd fallen to his knees, weeping woefully, afraid to go out there, until finally he had no choice but to close the door, the curtains—

His eyes.

Now, having looked again, he had no other options. He wiped away the tears, then raced around, resetting all the clocks to 2:55.

Mary would come soon.

And Mary came, Sweet Mary, the love of his life. He told her about his day, and he listened attentively to those details of the same repeating day she'd been living for thirty-three years. He wrapped her cookies for her, saw her to the door with closed eyes, bid her good night until tomorrow, then took the forgotten wrapped cookies to the kitchen. He smiled at the sight of ten-thousand-plus sets of wrapped cookies piled almost to spilling from the room. He loved her forget-fulness, how she never remembered to take her sugar-sprinkled star cookies home. He loved her earnestness, how she wanted to know about his life, the number of people living in the household, his age, his employment, his nationality . . .

That nice man from the church would be dropping off groceries again in a few hours. He hoped his benefactor would remember to bring sugar-sprinkled star cookies. Those were Mary's favorite.

Tomorrow Earnest P. Wittling would follow his practiced routine in preparing for Mary's daily three o'clock visit. This time he would remember to keep his eyes closed.

Mr. Wittling could always be in love . . . as long as he never looked too close.

Kitty Makes Three

I wrote this quite a while ago for posting on the old version of StephenGeez.com—back when it was a www. This story hasn't made it onto the new site—or onto the Fresh Ink Group site, for that matter—but now that the smoke has cleared, I think it's a fun romp that deserves a slot in this book. If anybody out there likes cats, maybe he or she would appreciate this tale about one. Thanks to Snake Wagner, who did the original acrylic painting that has been attached to the story ever since.

'm writing a list of ten.

They always prefer even numbers, but five is cool, too. I did have nine so far, but I needed #10 to achieve every editor's dream list, another in the rag-publishers' annals of "10 Steps to . . ." or "10 Ways You Can . . ." or "10 Things Every Woman Must . . ." I could have pared this one to eight—still an even number—but the assignment was ten, and trying to think of that last one is what nearly got me killed.

I stretched on the bed there in my new apartment, having finally earned enough by slogging articles and freelancing research to lease a place of my own—about time, for a guy pushing 25. (Despite my best efforts, Mom spotted my pseudonymous "10 Ways to Empty Your Nest" on a cover in the check-out line, its target the legions still housing and supporting live-at-home young'ns no longer so young.)

I closed my eyes and searched for inspiration amid the random firings of agitated rods and cones. All my thorough compilation had yielded nine good methods for a "10 Ways to Cut Your Food Bill" piece, but every idea for that elusive #10 proved laughably obvious. Sure, subsisting on buttered buttermilk biscuits in lieu of Chateaubriand would certainly reduce one's expenses, but consumers shelling out grocery money on point-of-purchase periodicals want to learn how they can eat braised beef on a buttered-biscuit budget.

My thoughts drifted to other self-help topics I might pitch, anything but how-to's involving pets. I didn't do pets, and I'd never quite mustered the empathy needed to imagine their owners' challenges so I could fashion a credible list of relevant advice.

That was before Katie cried.

The last thing I recalled of that brainstorming session was noticing the quiet, the solitude not only of inhabiting my own space, but of scoring a third-floor back-end unit in a building so new that for now boasted only one other tenant. I'd glimpsed but never met the young lady down the hall—Katie, according to the manager—a graduate student from out west, too busy pursuing a degree in veterinary science to show much interest in meeting new people.

So I lay there long enough to doze off, this I know because several "5 Ways to Prove You're Unconscious" hours had passed when I suddenly found myself in one of those "10 Ways to Protect Yourself In a Fire" dilemmas, the kind we all dread but never truly expect.

I couldn't breathe.

I had trouble seeing, too, the window light fading with dusk, probing gray smoke closing around me, but that breathing thing certainly ranked up there on any list of reasons to worry you might be about to die.

Even had I not written the fire-safety article, I would still assign rapid egress a spot near the top. My only alternative being over-the-balcony acrobatics, I opted for the mad-dash strategy. I grabbed a Step #3 wet towel for my face and threw on a Step #5 long coat with hood for flame protection, then stumbled into the smoke-choked hallway, keeping Step #8 low to the ground. I hadn't Step #1 planned and rehearsed my escape route, so I found myself banging into walls and tripping over my feet.

Yes, I lost my way and started freaking out, but in my defense I have two points to offer:

#1: I was trying to find the other tenant's apartment, and,

#2: You would have freaked, too.

I managed to find her door approximately twenty feet away, several miles from where I was visualizing it. Despite my brain urging immediate implementation of my get-the-hell-out plan—what some call the "flight reflex"—various parts attached to my butt all worked in concert to pound and kick that door.

Then I paused and listened, confirming the worst: faint sounds of movement, but no audible response to my fevered antics, likely a smoke-inhalation victim in distress.

So I started ramming the door with my shoulder, an entry method considerably more difficult and painful than is normally depicted on television and in films.

The door burst inward, and out flashed a glimpse of dark-gray cat that disappeared instantly amid of swirl of light-gray smoke. I rushed inside, shouted snotilly around my wet towel, Keystone Copped my way to a blurry-eyed survey of the bedroom and bathroom, then indulged my instincts for self-preservation.

I held the stairwell firedoor open long enough for the frenzied feline to flee, my own butt and its various attachments not far behind. I stumbled, tripped, got disoriented, and forgot all "12 Ways to Keep Your Wits in a Crisis."

Rubberized arms grabbed me and hustled me out to fresh, chilly air. I wiped my eyes in time to see that cat disappear into the adjacent woods, then started choking and coughing. Some EMT with an oxygen mask became my new best friend.

Crowds gathered, lights flashed, and the sky blackened with darkness that swallowed the smoke. The crowd's panic subsided as my rescuers determined nobody had failed to escape. Soon the captain announced the fire's demise, its footprint limited to the basement furnace area, living-level damage little more than smoke and soot spread through the ventilation system. Still, as a precaution, I would not be allowed access to my belongings for at least a day, so I headed for my car to sit and relax while pondering my "20-Point Checklist for Processing an Insurance Claim."

A bus stopped at the bus-stop out front. My neighbor burst out clutching her book bag, then broke into a frantic run toward the smoky building. I chased after her, soon gasping and winded, my head tingling, failing in my efforts to yell assurance—"Your cat, I let him out!" I caught up to her as a fireman blocked her from entering the building, but my tingling turned to a whirlwind of sparkles, and those rubberized arms had to catch me before I crashed face-first to the ornamental patio, contemporary paving-stone style #7.

"I let—your cat out," I gasped. "He's—okay."

"Where? Tell me! Please!"

"The woods! The woods!" I blurted, even as those rubber arms (and for this I'm grateful) held me steady.

"The woods?" I had confused her, a reaction quickly transformed to perplexity.

"He got away," I said defensively, and for some reason I found myself crossing that off some nebulous list of "Top 10 Ways to Impress a Lady."

She did look stunning, though. Her emerald eyes glistened in the streetlamp glow. Brush strokes of auburn-highlighted blond flowed in perfect symmetry around her features, a gentle nose begging to be nuzzled, full lips suggesting anticipation. Even in the overarching vulnerability of concern for her kitty, she hinted at the playful tease of a woman who knows men enjoy looking but most desire what they might yet discover.

"Show me?" she asked, her voice breaking now. The rubber arms let me stand on my own, and after the first tentative steps I managed to lead her past the spectacle of aftermath. Nothing about that smoky building mattered anymore as we found ourselves in darkness, wading through mud and muck, swiping at industrious mosquitoes, pausing here and there for her to call out.

"Carlysle!" she pronounced calmly, proximity her assurance, connection her promise. "Carlysle!" she called again, adding quietly to me, "He's never been outside."

"Carlysle J. Katt!" she called, her projection of confidence more forced now. I dared not speak lest the feline sense my deep-seated disdain for short hairy critters on four legs.

"I'm glad you let him out," she said. "Thank you." Sure, I had let him escape into the woods, but I saved his life. I was the hero in this picture. This would work out, thanks to me.

So we waited and listened, and I wanted to brush her temples lightly with my fingertips, then stroke her cheek with the back of my hand and move closer so our breaths would mingle, smoke and perfume. But what I wanted most was to see her holding her cat, relief in her eyes, everything better how, me promising her a copy of my "20-Point Checklist for Processing an Insurance Claim."

But Carlysle wouldn't appear, so we slogged through more mud, gazed expectantly into the blackness, and held our breaths to listen, her voice breaking the silence only to call again and again. I fetched a flashlight from my car, and we followed paths until woods turned to wetlands, and we got cold and dirty and frustrated and very worried about a darned animal.

And that's when Katie cried.

Construction materials piled too close to a furnace, and two people stood homeless in the light. I could always come up with at the least the first five ways to do something, but right then I couldn't even think of #1 on the list of "How to Flush Out a Scaredy Cat."

I stood close, hesitant to touch her, then reminded her he must be afraid, too, and maybe he just needed some time. She might falter in a moment of despair, but I would never let her give up. She had left her home, her family, her friends, and traveled across the country. She'd brought Carlysle, not just to look out for him, but so he could look out for her.

That's when I understood, and my own eyes filled with tears, too, which I still like to think was caused by the smoke, a natural response to expel airborne particulate, bodily homeostasis to maintain visual clarity.

I could see our breaths now, my hands stiff from the cold, a hint of rosy dawn backlighting the fire marshal's truck, crowd gone, road quiet. I wanted her to smile. I wanted to do whatever it takes to make Katie smile.

So I used her cellphone to call a friend of mine who produces music, rousing him before full daylight, #4 on the list of ways to aggravate even the best of friends. He grudgingly sampled a sound for me, burned it onto a CD, and drove it over.

So as the complex's residents emerged from the safety of their homes, they found a very odd site indeed: my car parked alongside the woods, engine off, Katie calling for somebody named "Carlysle," a CD in the stereo intermittently playing the sound effect of an electric can opener.

And that silly cat answered, a tentative meow at first, his fuzzy gray face peering out, not from the woods, but from under the trash bins adjacent to our smoke-damaged building.

He looked confused, tentative, even wary, but when she picked him up and nuzzled him, he purred.

I might have purred a bit, too, but don't quote me on that part.

That was the first of many times I played a part in making Katie smile. In the years since, I've still never written an article about animals, but I will someday, maybe "10 Ways a Pet Can Change Your Life." It's really too long a list, though, including how an animal can offer companionship for an elderly shut-in, teach children the responsibility of caring for another, protect us with warnings of intruders, and be the loyal friend you take along when it's time to travel far from home to study or work in a lonesome new place.

And sometimes a pet can even bring two people together.

So the final item on my "10 Ways to Cut Your Food Bill in Half" list turned out to be: "Cook for two." And when I wrote "12 Ways to Accidentally Meet Your True Love," I made #1 "When someone needs help, offer it unconditionally."

Editors always prefer the even numbers, but life plays by its own rules. When Katie and I found each other, two odd numbers did make an even. She laughed about that, then pointed out that Mr. Katt makes three.

So I'm still writing those lists, and with Katie expecting now, I figured our three would soon become an even four. But then Doc said something about twins. How cool is that?

We're already writing our own list of five.

Tailwind

My prompt for this is a photo taken by Scott Watson at the Henry Ford Museum in Dearborn, Michigan. I like Scott's work, so several of his photos have inspired stories of mine. I've never piloted an aircraft, and that seems unlikely to change, but I like to imagine how that must feel. I suspect it's something pilots can feel from time to time, even safely from the ground. Still, comes a time for us all when we really need a co-pilot.

"You know, Willie? I'm right pleased you're still flying with me."

"It's my pleasure, Jack."

"Hey, just how many times *have* we gone up together?"

"Well, I don't rightly know. I'd have to count 'em up."

"Don't really matter," Jack said, stealing a glance over at Willie. It never failed to amaze him how old his co-pilot was looking these days, especially for being the slightly younger man. They liked to spar about that every now and then—you old buzzard I ain't no buzzard but if I am you're an older one at least a buzzard gets to spend most of *his* time in the air.

Willie snorted, then got all quiet for a second. Finally, he admitted, "Well, what matters is, we always made it back down safe." He had a catch in his voice, which hinted at just one of the many reasons there wasn't another soul Jack would rather fly with. Willie never forgot what it was that first pushed 'em both skyward so long ago.

"As many flights as you captained," Jack said, "—well, I know there had to be a reason you'd still be willing sometimes to take second seat, that, uh, that you, um—" Damn, there was a catch in his own voice now. Enough of this nonsense. He directed his attention to the aircraft. "God, she's as sexy as they get, ain't she?"

Willie followed his gaze to the silver vixen tethered before them, the magnificent mighty DC-3. "Man, don't you just know it?"

"Finest aircraft Douglas ever assembled, that any wanderlusting soul ever conceived." Jack caressed her with his eyes, nose to wingtips to ailerons. Her silver skin shined, still smooth as that day she'd rolled off the line in Wichita, 360,000 rivets lovingly placed, every part machined to a work of art. They had dressed this one up for the old Northwest Airlines, orange-tipped props, eagle-winged cockpit windows, dual fuselage lightning stripes like Thor himself might dance with this goddess but never quite claim her for his own. And that nose, those engine cowlings—liquid cobalt, as if the pure blue juices dripped from her face after she'd drunk too many hearty drafts of cerulean sky.

Jack closed his eyes and whispered so no one but Willie could hear: "Let's take her up."

"Hmmm . . ." Willie responded, his way of saying well now let's think about that maybe another day might be better. "You know there's a bad storm coming," he whispered back, any words less than cocksure bravado best delivered on the QT.

"Well, I know that," Jack said, "But I think we can get above it, at least for a while, maybe find some tailwind to ride."

"Well then," Willie said, confidence returning to his voice, "it would be my pleasure, sir."

As soon as they lifted off, Jack felt it, that familiar vibration, a gentle rhythm that feeds the soul and glides in time to a true pilot's heartbeat. "They can keep their jet engines," he growled—swear words, for sure. "They work against you, or in spite of you." He never liked how jets devour the air, then cough it up, no respect wham bam thank you ma'am got what I come for I'll be on my way now. He continued, "I say give me a couple of fine-tuned Pratt Whitneys any time. They got respect for the sky, feeling for the jetstream, savoring God's air one slice at a time, then putting it back just the way they found it.

Willie chuckled and nodded the way he'd nodded a million times, that gleam in his eye saying I hear you and know exactly what you're talking about been there myself a few times yessiree Jack.

"Hey, Willie? Let's see if we can still find that wind."

The co-pilot tilted his head and bit his lip, his way of saying maybe not such a good idea let's think this through don't wanna go too far. "I'm worried about that storm coming," is what he said. "Maybe we should think about heading for home."

"I know I know," Jack said quietly. "I hear you, but how many more times we gonna get ourselves a chance like this? This is our plane, partner. She's built to *laugh* at storms, if only for a little while."

"Well, it's—" Willie started to say, but his words caught again.

Jack stole another glance and saw the old man next to him with an instant of clarity, that sparse fringe of hair tasseling the back of his uniform hat, deep grooves worn into the contours of a face that had seen its share of storms, eyes glistening with unrealized passion for soaring above man's limitations. No fear, though. Never afraid, always sure.

"It's your command, Captain," Willie said. "Take us in."

So Jack started climbing, higher, then higher yet, even as perspiration beaded under his visor, a rivulet or two snaking down the grooves of his own cheeks, his collar now damp. "You gotta feel it," he said reverently, barely loud enough to be heard over the roar of engines slicing cerulean sky. "Feel it in your hands, through your seat, running right into your body and through your very soul." He sighed, then closed his eyes. "You covering the instruments?"

"I'm right here," Willie answered.

"It's to the left—yes, port side, and up a ways. Feel her? She's pulling on the wing, making number one not have to work so hard." He eased the DC-3 portward, gently rising. "She's pulling us in," he said, barely stemming the excitement he felt.

"I *do* feel her," Willie said, also excited now.

And Jack found her.

He found the tailwind he'd chased every time he flew, his greatest moments in the sky realized when she'd take him for the ride. He backed off the throttle and embraced her, letting the wind carry them, their props just barely ahead of earth's every breath, just enough to keep the DC-3 aloft as two old men strapped in to surf the clouds.

But soon the turbulence slammed into them, their fickle tailwind cowed by forces greater than any man can face alone. Jack felt the storm pass through him, no plane powerful enough to hold them aloft forever.

"We need to set her down soon," Willie warned, sounding far away, but somehow right in Jack's ear.

"I—I don't feel so good," Jack said, bathed in sweat now, the fever coming faster, turbulence pummeling him unmercifully. "Willie?!" he called out, opening his eyes again, looking about frantically. "Willie?! I—"

"I got us, Jack," said his co-pilot. "I'm bringing us down. Just hold on; we're almost there."

He panted for breath. "It's—it's a bad—bad one."

"I got you," Willie said again, and Jack believed him, so many times he'd said I got you Jack it's okay don't worry I'll get you home we got people waitin' for us.

Another wave came over him, pushing him down hard, rolling him under as he gasped again, his skin hot, then clammy and cold.

Willie handed Jack a thick cloth, waiting while he wiped his brow, his neck, his face.

Jack covered his eyes with the cloth, rubbing gently, drying them lest somebody see. He breathed deeply, just a bit longer this time—or maybe not, hard to tell—and when he got his bearings straight he dropped the cloth, opened his eyes, and found himself on solid ground, Willie beside him, both gazing up at that magnificent, mighty DC-3, the finest aircraft Douglas ever assembled, that *any* wanderlusting soul ever conceived.

"Maybe next time?" Jack started, whispering again. "Maybe next time we could come here *before* the treatments?"

Willie gently took the cloth and stowed it in a satchel. "Well, this place doesn't open that early, but I think we might can try to get you a later slot at the clinic when one comes available."

"Yes. That would be better." Jack took a deep breath, then reached down and felt the wheel-bars. "I'm not—I'm still not feeling so good."

"I'll stay on point this time," kidded his co-pilot, "but next one's on you."

Jack reached up and patted Willie's hand as his lifelong friend wheeled him past a thousand exhibits, myriad visitors pausing to watch two old geezers in faded uniforms must be old-time pilots from back in the day hush now don't point. Willie pushed Jack down the long ramp, then out through the museum's double doors and into the lot, veering toward the handicap-parked van.

Cerulean sky stretched into the distance, a backdrop framing historic Dearborn's Greenfield Village, poignant moments from the past suspended against what sometimes dared to seem like limitless tomorrows. A gentle breeze stirred. Roiling storms still lay ahead, but plunging straight into them, knowing the right person is at your side, that's what helps most when the best you can do is close your eyes and ride them out.

Jack belted himself into the lightning-striped van, his face against the glass, eyes ever on the sky.

"You know, Willie? I'm right pleased you're still flying with me."

Family Treed

What I remember of this is that I felt playful, wanting to shift moods. This one is meant to poke fun at some stereotypical characters. The blatant frame of literary symbolism is so exaggerated, I got to make fun of that, too. Now, let's be clear: These characters are entirely fictional, though I can't deny visiting my own tree a time or two for inspiration.

In a meadow sliced by a deep limestone-cut stream, there on a gentle slope brushed with wildflower swaths, poses an exuberant old tree, its branches spread wide for scooping gobs of butter-yellow sunshine to fingerpaint the sky.

And one day Fred climbed that tree, quite nearly clear to the top.

Fred is a young man, quiet, what they call "taciturn," the kind of feller you know and count on without either of you having to say much, if anything, about it. He took custody of that tree when he bought Widow Harper's big old house, a gabled classic on one side of the stream, that tree on the other. A winding gravel road swung right past the wraparound porch before narrowing to a chert path connected by footbridge to the other side. From there another trail led the half-mile to Highway 96 and that ramshackle shack called the Dinger Place.

Crissy Dinger had a lot to do with why he came to move there. After barely six months of sparking, he married her, giving her a home not ten minutes' walk from seeing her mama, Granny Bess, anytime she wanted, not to mention those three shiftless older brothers, Cousin Cindy with the cosmetology certificate she never uses, and Cindy's teenage twins, a swish of a boy who looks and acts like a girl and a supersized girl known for not being the type who likes boys. Not six months after that, she ran off with Lester from the feed store—somewhere out west, they say—certainly farther than ten minutes by footbridge and a chert path from her kinfolk.

The day Fred climbed that big old tree, he had me out there to run a backhoe for him. I figured he wanted to dig somewhere, but he didn't say, and with Fred you kinda figure there isn't any reason to talk about it till the hoe arrives and time comes to start digging. Problem was, some feller over in Buchananville was using it, so Cyrus couldn't haul it to Fred's place until it came available. We had plenty of time to kill.

Fred studied across the bridge and up the hill, checked his watch, and motioned me into the parlor. We uncapped a couple of beers and parked ourselves in front of the news channel. Not five minutes passed before Granny Bess no-knocked her big old lunk of a self right through the front door like she held an engraved invitation, her older boy and Cindy's twins right behind her.

"Brung the beer," she announced, waving a six-pack with three bottles already drained. She heaved herself into the big recliner while Lazy Son stretched out to wallow on the long couch, muck-crusty shoes and all. "Well?" she barked. "I need openin'."

Girly-Boy flounced off toward the kitchen, Burly-Sis rolling her eyes before following. Girly-Boy hurried back, top-popped all three beers, then disappeared into the kitchen again.

"*Wheel*'s on," Granny Bess announced, grasping for the remote, cursing under her breath when she couldn't quite reach it. Needing to sit up, she swiped it off the coffee table. Fred never said a word when she proceeded to flip through the channels until she found that Sajak feller grinning at Vanna.

The twins returned with armfuls of food: sodas, bags of chips and pretzels, a tub of dip, some kind of sausage for Girly-Boy to gnaw on. Lazy Son drained his beer and eyed the last full one, but Granny Bess shot him a look, so he shrugged and headed for the kitchen, returning with two more from Fred's supply. The twins fought over who would sit where until Girly-Boy spilled chips all over the floor and Burly-Sis slapped him for it, which made the boy tune up and cry like a sissy girl. Granny Bess hollered threats at both young'ns, then at Cousin Cindy when she waltzed right in and plopped down, showing no interest in controlling her heathen brats.

Nobody acknowledged me, Fred's company. Come to think of it, Fred didn't seem to register any more of their take-notice than a dried cowpie in a pasture would, either.

Wasn't long before Ugly Son showed up. Tall and skinny, he didn't look any better than the last time I saw him, a kid back then, in the school parade. Imagine somebody with a face touched up by a baseball bat, decorate it with angry pimples verging on open boils, and you'd be picturing somebody two shudders and a cringe handsomer than this feller. I mean, seriously, look away—which I tried to do, but he kept glaring at me as if I must be squatting in his seat. Finally, he claimed the antique-looking chair by the fireplace and snapped his fingers at the twins. Burly-Sis rolled her eyes, but Girly-Boy obediently bolted for the kitchen, then traipsed back with an open beer and a bowl of something or other. If you think you know ugly, wait till you try to stomach watching ugly eat.

When the *Wheel* rerun ended, a cacophony of cussing and rank-pulling ensued, the result a compromise between Granny Bess and Lazy Son, a channel offering some kind of bass-fishing show. Without a sound, Fred repaired to the kitchen, returning with another beer each for himself and me. I didn't want to drink too much before running a backhoe, but Ugly Son kept challenging me with the vermin eye, so I figured deepening the old barley-and-hops stream would help keep him beyond the opposite bank.

A lot of rather pointed questions sloshed around in my head, but I didn't ask them 'cause I didn't want to have to listen to the people who might answer.

I could see that what little bit of temper Fred might have had started to steam like a microwave burrito, but still he never said a word, never made eye contact with a one of them.

Three or four bass-catches into the program, Loud Mouth barged in to join the crowd. The youngest son, he might have been old enough to buy liquor, or maybe not. He had a reputation around town for having an opinion on everything, for not knowing much about anything, and for running his mouth constantly to prove both. He started in about something the mayor had done or was going to do or maybe said he was thinking about doing, but everyone ignored him except Granny Bess; she responded to his prattle, all right—by turning up the TV. By then, the twins had started fighting, Girly-Boy crying again, so Lazy Son actually put enough space between his backside and the couch to reach out and slap them both. That triggered a free-for-all in which Burly-Sis nearly whipped his tail. Ugly Son responded by heading toward the kitchen to open more beers and make sandwiches. Girly-Boy quit crying long enough to follow and fetch himself a box of sugar cereal, which he ate by the handful, spilling bits on the furniture and floor. Granny Bess told Loud Mouth to shut up, no way do those bass shows fake it with rubber fish, now go heat me something in the microwave. Cousin Cindy slipped her nail file into a pocket, adjusted her too-tight bra, and disappeared down the hallway, something about needing to take a wicked pee. Lazy Son farted, long and loud, earning giggles from Girly-Boy.

I don't know about you, but in Fred's stead my druthers would be to boot their butts right out the door. I mean, seems like they're really not even kinfolk anymore—Crissy leaving him had sawed off that branch of the family tree—and they sure didn't know how to make themselves welcome like company in somebody else's house. Worse, I had a feeling this was every day's business. Freeloading, is what we call that where I come from; and since I'm from just up Highway 96, I'm pretty sure that's what they call it here, too.

Granny Bess took a bite of whatever Ugly Son brought her from the microwave. She twisted her face into a grimace, talking with her mouth full as she described it in excretory terminology while cramming it back into the wrapper and tossing it onto the coffee table.

That's when Fred made his move.

I mean, I wasn't sure what he was doing at first. He just stood up, looked around until he roused everybody's curiosity, then headed out toward the woodshed. Not wanting to be left alone with a roomful of varmints, I followed in silence, Girly-Boy trailing behind.

Fred retrieved an aluminum extension ladder from the shed, along with some kind of canvas harness or hammock or something or other attached to the end of a long braided rope. He walked down the trail, crossed the footbridge, then veered left off the path and headed straight for that big old tree by the water, stepping high through the tall grass.

He leaned that ladder against the tree, pulled the cable until the extension fit tightly between two big branches, and proceeded to climb. He draped the rope and harness over a low branch, then continued upward, nothing difficult about it, until he reached as near the top as one can get, some hundred feet or more off the ground.

Girly-Boy watched, then eyed me for a minute before rushing back to the house. Soon the whole group spilled out into the yard, drinks in hand, milling about and mumbling among themselves.

When Loud Mouth announced, "He's up to something," the increasingly restless herd shifted gradually toward the water, craning for a better look. We could all see Fred up there, but leaves obscured our view, exactly what he was doing unclear.

I headed downstream, crossed the footbridge, and walked up close enough to see better. Fred simply sat up there, sometimes looking around, sometimes gazing off across the horizon. Noticing me below, he acknowledged me with a nod before looking away. I found a seat in the grass off to the side, sitting back against a large boulder to watch.

Granny Bess and Ugly Son went back to the house and disappeared inside for several minutes, but out they came again, a six-pack of open beers to hand out. Finally they anointed Lazy Son to cross the bridge and head for the tree. He peered into the branches, then turned toward the group and shrugged.

Not satisfied, Granny Bess dispatched her other two sons. The twins followed, Cousin Cindy a few minutes later. A spirited debate ensued, not about Fred's intent, but over who would head up into the tree for a better look. Finally, Granny Bess charged across the bridge and joined the pack, their alpha female taking charge.

Ugly Son got the nod, but since Lazy Son and Loud Mouth both wanted the honor, too, they followed close behind, then more or less raced each other up through the branches. Burly-Girl had been chafing at not being considered for the job, so she set off on her own trek toward the top, choosing the more precarious routes as if to demonstrate her prowess. Girly-Boy wanted to go, too, but seemed a bit scared until Cousin Cindy teased him and he teased back and both eventually goaded each other to prove their worth by going up.

"Get closer, and find out what that lunatic thinks he's doin'!" Granny Bess ordered, ground control nudging flights toward a collision course.

Two generations filled the branches, but nobody worked up the gumption to say a word to Fred. You ask me, I think they knew he wouldn't answer, so they feigned some measure of dignity in acting like they didn't want to know.

Ten minutes passed, fifteen, twenty . . . Eventually Granny Bess hollered, "You boys get down here and help me."

Now, Fred must have been thinking ahead, I'll give him that. The next fifteen minutes proved to be some of the funniest I've ever seen, mainly because Bess's boys wound up having to use that harness and hundred feet of braided rope to help her flail and cuss her way up to a crotch of wide branches where she could wedge. Here I'm thinking I sure don't want that backhoe to arrive anytime soon, because I want to keep my seat for part two of this show. Anybody who's ever scaled an obstacle knows that getting down is twice as hard as climbing up.

"It's the view," Cousin Cindy pronounced. "Ain't it pretty? You can see clear across the four hills and over to Buchananville. He come up here for the view."

"He didn't climb all that way for no look at no town," Granny Bess scoffed.

"He's watching the animals!" Girly-Boy gushed. "See the mama bird on her nest? Look, two squirrels watching us from over there." He picked something off a branch. "See? I got a cala-piller."

Burly-Sis scoffed at that. "No, he's gonna steal them bird's eggs, cook 'em or hatch 'em and raise 'em to eat."

Ugly Boy disagreed. "He's got somethin' hid up here, and we caught him before he could get to it."

"He's just showing off," Granny Bess pronounced. "Good for nothin', trying to prove he can do somethin'."

"Prob'ly gonna jump," Lazy Son offered, a bit too much enthusiasm at the notion in his voice. "Do his self in."

Cousin Cindy suggested, "Maybe he's looking to see where he wants to trim some branches."

"I know," said Loud Mouth. "I heard tell he's got a backhoe comin' from Cyrus. He's lookin' to see where to dig a hole."

"What's he diggin' a hole fer?" Granny Bess demanded to know.

"He's gonna plant something!" Girly-Boy exclaimed.

"Or bury somebody," his twin supplied.

Right then a backscatter of dust like the smoke off an old train worked its way down the gravel road, the rumble of a truck soon drowning out the birds. By the time anybody noticed, Fred had climbed down out of that tree. He collapsed the ladder and hoisted it, then footed his way through the tall grass, across the footbridge, and up to the shed. That big old tree came alive with noise, a whole covey of Dingers not liking the idea of being trapped with no ladder. Seems now everybody did have something to say to Fred, quite a shift in the wind from sitting in his house, ignoring him while helping themselves to his stores. The truck drowned 'em out, though, as Cyrus pulled in and parked; and the diesel on that backhoe made a bigger noise as I drove it off the trailer. Fred came out and gestured simple instructions for the job, then headed back inside, no interest in sticking around to watch.

Turns out he didn't want to do any digging at all.

So it took all of ten minutes, and I pulled the backhoe back onto the trailer as the last splintered beams of that footbridge floated down the stream. I knocked on Fred's door. He greeted me with a handshake and a grin, inviting me inside.

He'd already cleaned up the mess, set out some snacks, opened us a couple of beers. We sat around for hours swapping stories, more words out of Fred than I'd ever heard.

"Been a long time," he said, "since I had comp'ny."

He has me by the place every other week or so now, maybe to play cards or sit around with Cyrus and those fellers from the feed store. I've met his new lady-friend a couple of times, too, when he brings her back this way instead of driving over to Piderboro where she lives with her mama and two brothers.

Sometimes I'll stop on that gravel road and listen for the cackle of wild Dingers up among the branches, but I know they're back in their own ramshackle house, no point in coming down to the water anymore, no way to cross. Fred's thinking about holding his wedding right there at his place come next spring. Right outside would be nice, there in that meadow by the deep, limestone-cut stream.

I can picture it now: in the background you'll see a gentle slope brushed with wildflower swaths, an exuberant old tree posing for the photos, its branches spread wide for scooping gobs of butter-yellow sunshine to fingerpaint the sky.

Bus, Boy

The comma in the title belongs there, not that its omission would wreck anything. I used to work as a busboy at Andre's age. I thought about that one day with fondness for some of those people who first respected, then befriended me. A lot of the young employees learned and matured from the experience. More than a few didn't. I thought I might write about that. Any similarities to real people, living or dead, are most assuredly meant with fondness and tribute.

Busboy.

André, the punk-ass busboy.

Scratchy black pants, stiff white shirt, cheap dark shoes. Sixteen years old, embarrassed to be here, he sits in a booth in the back, waiting for paperwork and some here's-what-you-do.

P.O. set this up, said only way outta this place is to find a better job hisself. Got tomorrow and the next day off before a five-day schedule kicks in. *Bet* he'll have something better before having to show his face for a second day in *this* place. Judge said gotta work full-time now, then part-time and GED classes in the fall, or serve that suspended year. Catch another case and he's gone for even longer. That was last week. Probably shoulda started looking for his own job then.

Moms cried when she showed him the clothes she bought him— proud of him, she said, bring in some money, help out, maybe get some insurance to share her car. Teenage boys cost a lot.

Restaurant-style food joint in the mall, booths and tables and stools at a counter, waitresses running trays, two cooks behind the lights, order slips clipped to a turning-deal, Lenore at the register on your way out. It's humiliating, working at a place like this, these kinda people, right by home where everybody he knows can see him. P.O. says people respect honest work. Yeah, right.

Ain't no respect here: cleaning up after slobs, bussing tables, washing dishes, working like a dog, customers lined up hurry hurry hurry up wipe that down get the seats. Waitresses gotta make that money.

Lenore brings the papers. Sour old bitch doesn't like him already, that mean look on her face, wasting her time on a punk she can tell won't be back after today. Got that right. Fill this out here and here and sign there and both of these. Punch in here, but not till it's time. Aprons in the box. Wilbur here'll show you what to do.

Wilbur, now that's some piece of work. He's, like, ninety years old, probably retarded, too. Lives his whole life, and this is all he's done for himself? Dale's the other busboy, eighteen or nineteen, just leave him alone and stay out of his way. Dale seems really cool, making the best of it, moving too fast for anyone to notice who he is.

Wilbur takes forever explaining what to do. How hard can it be? Like, stack dishes in the gray tubs—not too loud—then wipe everything down with a clean-looking rag. Leave tip-money on the table. *Don't mess with the tips.* Waitresses will pick 'em up, except sometimes they leave good ones there long enough for the next group to see what's expected. "Greedy bitches," Dale calls 'em.

Filling the gray tubs, wiping up people's mess, shoving tubs through the window, loading dishes in the racks, spraying off the mess, putting racks in the washer, stacking hot dishes, hauling stacks to the kitchen and waitress stations.

Dale likes to empty his own tubs, and André finally figures why. Dale sometimes fishes a quarter out the bottom, maybe two dimes. He's slick until you know what to watch for. Wipes the table, pushes the money aside, covers a coin or two with the rag, slides it into his tub. Anybody ever sees it—oops, sorry. Working too fast. My bad.

New guy better lay low for a while, though, everybody watching to see how he works, see if he's going to last. Wilbur keeps telling him good job good job, like what that old man thinks matters.

Waitresses slip into the back for quick breaks, bathroom, a few bites, sips of Diet Pepsi. They introduce themselves to the new boy: Hi, sugar, I'm Loretta Cindy Tisha Jean Emma Abigail. Each offers advice, acts friendly, grateful he's looking out for her section. Don't worry about Lenore. She'll be on you for messing up, but when you do your best she looks out for you. Abu's the owner, mostly stays in the office, pushing piles of paper and complaining how keeping this place open is a miracle.

Tisha comes back, calls her sister. Can you watch the kids again tomorrow? Got offered an extra shift. She looks up and sees André watching, looks embarrassed. Got two little ones, she says, running up doctors' bills on the youngest, money hard to come by. Don't get to spend much time with her babies for working so hard to take care of her babies.

André's mom has said something like that once or twice.

And now he's stacking dishes in the gray tub and feeling kinda not cool about asking Moms for money all the time, about that look on her face when she digs through that purse, calculating what she absolutely needs, what she can spare, then hands him more than she can afford. She cried when he got popped, worried about money for a lawyer, wondering what she'd done wrong or didn't do right.

And he's wiping down the tables, eyeing that money, moving it around with his clean-looking rag, thinking how some extra quarters, maybe two dimes here and there would add up, a way to hand his check to Moms and still keep some for himself; but Tisha appears, helping him wipe the seats, her table in her section, a chance to grab that good-tipping group next in line if André finishes before Dale gets Loretta's booth ready. Tisha's quarters pay doctors' bills.

And that smug-ass P.O. shows up, sits at the counter, eats chocolate pie, smirks while André busses the counter, never says a word. Yeah, come by next week for more pie, won't see this guy here. One day as Lenore's dog and he's through. *Any* job's better than this.

People from down the street come in, recognize André. The mom and dad and little girl and that boy in eighth grade. They smile, offer a wave on the down-low, keep looking at the dog running around, cleaning up after others. Real low class.

But when André busses the next booth over, the man stands up, sticks his hand out and shakes, respect in his eyes. Good to see you've become a working man, he says; and the eighth-grader wants to know how old he's got to be to get a job here someday, make his own money. Girl thinks André's pants and shirt look cool.

And the line grows longer, the pace picking up, everybody frantic, money to be made. Some customers come by to look, then decide the wait is too long. That takes money off the tables, leaves doctors' bills unpaid. Abu's running the register now so Lenore can work the stations, fill glasses and plate desserts and make salads so the waitresses move faster. Lenore doesn't even *get* tips, but it's like she wants to make sure her girls make every dime they can. Dale's working like a blur, throwing glances at André, a challenge. Some of the girls look pleased when Dale gets to their tables first; André's not turning 'em over fast enough.

But, see, André's smart, and he spots ways to be quicker: two hands, spare rags, half and half, double-tubbing, lots of possibilities. Just like that, everybody's impressed, and Wilbur can stay in the back, keep the racks moving. Cooks are slinging like a blur, order slips spinning that turn-deal, Abu punching keys and counting change and maybe, just for a minute, not worrying about how this place stays open.

And Dale's going straight to the pocket now, a quick belly-scratch under his apron, but André can see what's up.

Wilbur keeps looking out that little window, hungry for more tubs. Lost his wife, Tisha whispered over sips of Diet Pepsi earlier. Doctors' bills, funeral costs, needed money at first, but now maybe it's something to do, someplace to go. Even stops by on his days off, she says, hangs out for a bit when it's slow. Everybody likes Wilbur. Don't even think about giving him a hard time; Lenore'll make you wish you were somewhere else.

The rush eases a bit, and Diane Stapleford comes in with her mom, booth in the back. He's had it for her since, like, sixth grade, but she never gives him a look, too good for him.

Except now she's looking hard, watching him, smiling and winking whenever she catches his eye. Her mom whispers something to her, and they both giggle, Diane blushing.

Come over and watch a movie, she says when he's close by. And suddenly the humiliation of working like a dog in scratchy black pants and stiff white shirt looks more like just being a responsible person, like acting grown up, like a young man looking after his mom, a young man who would look after his girl someday.

And Abu calls Dale into the office, the bigger cook and Lenore right behind him. Other cook takes Dale's coat from the back and hands it in. And Wilbur watches it all through that little window, looking sad like someone hurt him bad. That old man's about ready to cry, like everything's his fault, like he didn't show Dale the right way to do this job.

Like it hurt him to be the one had to say something to the boss.

And Dale's out the door, cussing and flashing the bird. The waitresses look sad but relieved.

Tisha's the first one to clock out. She catches André in the back and whispers how proud she is of him, then presses eight dollars into his palm before grabbing her coat and hugging Wilbur on the way out.

Loretta slips a bunch of ones into his shirt pocket, Cindy a roll of dimes, Jean a five-dollar-bill. One of the cooks brings him and Wilbur big plates, sandwiches and onion rings and garlic pickles.

Emma and Abigail come off another five apiece, but they stay to help clean up, fill ketchup bottles, rack pies, load machines, set up morning coffee, wrap silverware. Abu comes out from the office, looks around, makes eye contact with the new busboy for the first time. He nods, then heads back to the office.

And Wilbur looks proud.

But André's thinking about Diane Stapleford, about watching a movie and telling her about this crazy place and double-tubbing and Wilbur and Tisha and how Lenore's not really so mean.

And Lenore comes into the back, says she knows André probably has plans tomorrow, like she can read his mind about looking for a better job. Still, with Dale gone now, they're short-handed.

Can you work tomorrow? Lenore wants to know. Maybe next day, too?

André's mom sure could use some help on the money-tip. And André thinks maybe he could take Diane someplace tomorrow after work—and pay their way.

Emma and Abigail are watching, hoping he'll say yes.

P.O. made him come here, but now these people want him to come back. Scratchy black pants, stiff white shirt, cheap dark shoes, sixteen years old.

Eleven o'clock tomorrow.

André the busboy.

Working man.

Comes this Time to Float

I wrote this story to accompany a photo taken for me of a favorite waterfall. I titled it "Water Falls" and published it several places. I named this book after a different story. Then I decided to include this "Water Falls" story instead of "Float," so I simply renamed this story to match the book title. Yeah, it runs that deep—pun intended. Still, it's a very serious story, allegorical metaphor, using only one of the many ways this title can and should be interpreted.

Water falls.
Sun rises. Trees reach. Blooms lure. Birds call.
People connect.
An old woman drives muddy spoors, dual-tracked ruts wending through dense undergrowth. High-fiving branches scrape paint, her

cute little coupe ill-suited for penetrating dark forest deep in the peninsula above that mighty bridge. Magician's-box swords of sharp sunlight stab the gloom. Leaves turn and reach. An urgent rivulet slaps rocks. Water falls.

A log blocks her way. Brush fills gaps. Scattered trash looks embarrassed. No space to turn around, she kills the engine, then steps out and locks the doors, pretending it might somehow deter thieves here where nobody watches or listens. Even such pretenses of prudence and precaution ease need to worry, at least until bigger fears remind and distract.

Seventy-one, surely too old to hike alone, she carries her water bottle, plus fanny-packed snack, keys, and ID. No casual stroll, this way takes her where she needs to go.

Sporadic ruts narrow to barely discernible foot-trail. Stopping to rest on a large stone, she remembers. The dank rot of composting earth settles in her belly, worms rising in the gently turned soil of her grandparents' garden, buried seeds sensing their time to reach for light. Pine pollen tickles her nose and teases her throat, that dense stand of regal evergreens climbing the hill behind their cabin, brown needles shagging the carpet of forest floor, cones in a rubbish fire popping like firecrackers and Indian corn.

And the water.

Dew-drops and leaf-drips and mud-trickles and stone-polishing streams—she can taste them all. The river calls, its skulking mist probing the shadows, reaching out, reminding. A single droplet from that first summer at Grammie and Grampie's getaway has circled the world her whole life, but now it finds its way back, back to the river, back to the waterfall, back to what she knows.

She never expected to see this place again, but the phone rang and words stunned. She stopped eating. Two days passed. Empty inside, she searched inward for connection, then faced the truth and drove all night—pricey gas, cheap motel, stale bagel, warm shower, somber clothes, polite comments, a glance into that long polished box, tears falling even though nothing real about him still dwelled in the part they had dressed up and laid out. Expected to linger and pay ritual respects, she fled instead to the woods, begging him to save her, knowing he could no longer try.

Maybe she has a plan, but dares not wonder what it might be, the simplest way to avoid summoning those lurking fears.

A fat beetle trundles past her foot. Leaves rustle. Water drips.

She wonders if anybody else ever rested on this isolated rock, some lost soul pausing to watch and listen until lonesomeness grows unbearable, that illusion of being the only one left so real now that even crowds make it that much worse. A solemn procession of cars is wending its way toward the distant rise south of town, but she hurries deeper into the woods, pushing herself too hard.

Breaths labor. Heart pounds. Squirrels pause to watch and wait.

Will she ever find the river, ever find the falls? She tries to forget worries about diagnoses, money, incapacity, obligations, indifferent caretakers neglecting what remains of the man she married and sometimes even loved, who kept her even though their babies never lived, who accepted—without truly understanding—her long-distance friendship with that other man who always somehow remained the boy she met across the river that summer they both celebrated their tenths.

She pushes on, exhaustion helping her forget.

Perspiration beads and trickles. Water sings. Mists encircle.

And tea-colored river suddenly appears, right there, swift and cold, telling her she's found her way back. Locks on 36-payment car doors don't matter now because she will never leave this place.

She picks her way along the bank and finds where the cabin had stood until raging fires consumed it some four decades ago. The forest reclaimed its land, covering it with new growth, leaving scant telltale signs. There, a tumble of rocks betrays the old cistern. Across the water, pinkish stone slabs rise toward the ghost of long-missing swing-bridge, an unconfirming insinuation that three more cabins might once have lined the low ridge. She pictures the smallest, far right, where he'd come that summer with his uncle to celebrate, not just his first double-digit birthday, but the luck in a childhood nurtured by uncontested love. Never had he felt alone or worried nobody would care; and from that first meeting until his last breath, he'd given her the same assurance, especially when she could find it nowhere else, even when they forgot to talk.

Crickets summon. Birds argue. Temperature rises.

The river still looks familiar, except its red rocks and slabs of rose shale have been pushed around, the furniture rearranged. Distracted the time they first met, family quarrels and broken promises weighing hard, she slipped and plunged in, thrashing wildly, swept away. That brown-haired boy with the mischievous cowlick jumped after her, but instead of pulling her out, he simply held on and let the water take them, teaching her feet-forward, butt-down, hands-ready, eyes-wide. If you fight the pull, it'll give you to the rocks; trust it, and it will carry you on.

He kept her head above water again three months later when she called cross-country to cry about Daddy having gone, then for many summers afterward as they body-surfed the rapids, there in the river where she learned how to forget fear, if only for a time.

Friends take turns letting go of everything but one another, floating through those moments of trusting the other to watch for rocks.

Water never worries. Water collects, water flows, water falls.

She wants to slip in right now, to let the current carry her away, to prove that no one remains who can save her . . . but not here. This is not the place. She climbs over brush, then ducks branches, following the river, still fascinated by how fluid determination always finds its way. Water needs no one.

Her sixteenth year, winter stretched too long while anxiety loomed too large, and when she couldn't fight it anymore, she resorted to hurting herself, only a few times, not too much to keep secret. The realness of that pain, the confirmation in a smear of blood, had proven more manageable than relentlessly dreading the unknown; but even that never seemed as true as riding the river, and the next morning always brought with it even greater anxiety, the secret terror of knowing she came that much closer this time, so close to going too far.

Only he discovered what she had done, and seeing the scars made him cry. It never occurred to her that he could be afraid of anything, but in his eyes she saw not fear for himself, not for the friend he loved, but for the realization that sharp rocks can hide deep inside, that maybe no amount of feet-forward butt-down hands-ready eyes-wide could save her, and that a time might come when even he might fail to hold her head above water. She took his innocence that day, but he proved then and for the fifty-odd years since that he would never let her ride the currents alone, even when a thousand miles kept them apart, even living separate lives in different worlds.

Now she stands before the river. Tears fall, blurring the vision even as they focus the memory. How different is a naive young teen embracing pain to fight fear, from an old woman chasing her fears in a bid to end the pain?

She moves along until she recognizes those stairstep pools descending toward the falls. A long-forgotten but still-familiar roar reverberates from the sunken glen below. The final upper pool is widest, flat and serene, unsuspecting of what fate awaits its waters. It reflects the wispy white clouds, their blue backdrop tinting the tannin-stained surface, its rocky bottom lost and irrelevant, dark danger masked by the misleading reassurance of light. Rose-colored shale piles along the shore, then channels the overspill through several low spots where glassy lips disappear into rising mist. Vivid green backdrop shimmers in the distance.

A dejected tangle of cut and broken branches points to where someone cleared a campsite. She pulls two from the pile and tosses them in, watching until the ripples smooth. They appear unmoving until she sights them against objects on the far shore. Some people spend their whole lives floating in deceptive stillness; others never look away from those distant rocks, constantly gauging their progress, their loss.

Branches float. Water pulls.

She picks her way down a stony foot-trail that skirts the drop, layers of mossy shale like a funhouse staircase, occasional loose slabs offering unexpected rides.

Stepping into the open, she beholds a wondrous scene, a spectacular waterfall, several deeper flows, liquid the hues of paint-brush rinse where sunlight penetrates its mystery. One giant pool agitates furiously under the impact, then quickly ripples out to blunt its rage. Splitting into several rivulets, it drops into smaller pools that eventually converge so the river may continue on, discombobulated by such distraction, resolute in its journey. Stacked ledge-rock sentries signal their vigilance, splashes of pink and white wildflowers punctuating their warning, a panorama vivid with lush greens aglow in the yellowing sunlight.

No other person can be seen or heard. This morning, the falls belong to her.

All her life she has been fascinated by waterfalls, writing poems and painting pictures to explore the hold they exert on mortals. For her, it's the violence, the sudden drop, the notion that everybody rides the river and must inevitably succumb to its power, no one soul strong enough to worry the current every minute of life. It's an admission that letting go leaves no choice but to hope for the best, and that even glassy pools deceive with the illusion of serenity that can suddenly spill into incalculable void. In movies, the hero is pulled headlong into the surge, no way to see what lies beyond, an image that eventually cuts to a confirming view from below, the revelation, an instant of knowing how it turns out. People will sit for hours and watch the falls, losing themselves in so much raw power that never ends, awed by the notion that more and more water keeps coming, helpless but to meet its fate.

And she sees one of the branches she threw in, easing toward the spill, then suddenly sacrificed to the maelstrom. It plunges into the depths and disappears. She holds her breath to give it time, but the branch is held under until she simply must gasp for air. She tries again and again, knowing she would die a thousand deaths until finally, its confidence dashed, the battered remnant of a once-vibrant life gently surfaces and begins a slow circuit drifting around the eddies.

She swam here many times with him, then sat in sunshine and gazed upon all that violence while sun dried their shorts and warmed their goose-bumped skin. They never ventured any farther downstream, content to know this river surely flows on, that it passes under a highway several miles below, then continues its journey chasing successive horizons. Their last summer together, with no way to see what lies beyond, they explored their physical passions until surge took them unbidden; but the plunge that seized their breaths proved friendship can plummet, too, leaving them vulnerable in ways youth is so often too young to understand. Thereafter, they chose to limit their love to the stretch that felt safe, to float with confidence and portage the unknown, to linger where innocence still pooled, always alert to the undertow.

People drown under waterfalls.

They cannot be saved. Those who dive after them meet the same fate.

That boy, the one who used to warn her about the rocks, died an old man in his easy chair, starting a letter, they say, to his lifelong friend, his unwritten words forever lost. The grief is more than she can bear, the uncertainty in looming challenges too great to face alone. Now the indifferent power of these falls will claim the life of a lonesome and scared old woman, her own unconsidered memories forever lost.

She lays her water bottle and fanny pack on the rocks, then rubs her eyes, determined to be strong even when she goes under. Dying in the depths allows water to absorb one's tears, even as it scrubs the blurring stain of loss.

She steps in, then wades deeper. Bitter cold seizes her breath, wrapping her in liquid embrace. Then it bears down, squeezing the woman whose loves have all gone, the woman whose husband is reduced to little more than a broken limb drifting eddies with no memory or recognition, the woman told her diagnosis might be overcome but the regimen of treatments would be hard, sharp challenges inevitably exacting a harsh price.

And nobody remains to hold her head.

Suddenly the bottom falls away.

That boy had looked into her heart sixty-one years ago, then proved over a lifetime that no other could see what even she never dared show. How could he leave her now, when she needs him most, lost to the water she had always known would take her?

She dips below surface. Icy cold shivers her violently, slashing pain making her decision more real.

Undertow pulls her in. The old man reminds her how that boy used to worry she might swim too close, the way he always stayed near, ready to reach out, even when a thousand miles and different worlds kept them apart.

She bobs to the surface, surprised to find air, scared another breath will breathe new life into flourishing regrets. This is not over yet.

Spray blinds her.

The power pulls her back under.

All she can see in the tannin-colored swirl is his face, the way he looked that day when he finally understood she truly tried to hurt herself, the way it made him cry, the way he started fearing what might happen to her, the realization that now he would always have to worry.

She tries to gasp, but chokes in the water. She kicks and thrashes and fights in a final bid, this time, to save him, now realizing what he wanted to say in that unfinished letter, what he's been saying all these years.

What he's saying even now.

Rocks bark her legs. Waves slap her face. She reaches for him, but knows this time she must hold her own head above water.

She kicks with every bit of love she can summon. More than her own, it is the love from another that buoys her.

Her arm tangles in a branch. It tugs her, so she follows it into the current. She catches an outflow and spills from the brink into calmer water along the side, the gentle nudge of eddy urging her clear.

Her husband needs her, and though he's forgotten who she is, he descended into darkness believing she would always keep his head up. He would have done that for her. Promises can only be honored by those left to keep them.

She tries to swim, but is too exhausted, so she gives in and floats, letting the water take her.

Sun rises high. Swords of bright light stab trees. Iridescent damselflies flit.

He wanted to remind her one last time, but she had to come back here to be sure.

The water eases her toward the downstream flow.

He wanted to say he cannot hold her forever. He knew the time had come, no choice but to let go. Trust the water. Feet-forward, butt-down, hands-ready.

Eyes-wide, it's a glorious ride.

She climbs onto rocks and wipes her face, then beholds the spectacular scene, the way it reminds, the way it remembers.

She rests awhile, mourning her friend as legions have long struggled to cope, then picks her way over to the side and retrieves her water bottle, her fanny pack. Shielding her eyes from glare, she looks again toward the outflow, and notices those two broken tree branches now pulled into the lower river, coasting between rocks, under trees, toward more falls and the highway that takes so many home.

It breaks her heart, the admission that one journey has ended; but it is that lifetime of friendship, every minute cherished, that helped bring her this far. The water can never claim these tears. Shed for him, they will always belong to her.

She hurries closer to watch the branches disappear around a bend, the way they never hesitate to accept their fate. Maybe they, too, are curious to see where it flows, what still waits ahead.

Her car is the other way, but if she can get to the highway, surely there will be a ride. People are always willing to help. People connect. People remember. People know.

People make *new* promises.

She turns back for one more look at the falls, and she knows she will never return to this place. Water never climbs.

She closes her eyes and bids her friend farewell, then vows never to squander the gift he left her.

Rocks shine. Trees reach. Blooms lure. Birds call.

She finds the trail and pushes on, following the river.

Water falls.

Survivors go on.

The Age-Eater

For the penultimate tale in this collection, I'm offering one more from a fantasy realm. Really not much of a fantasy writer myself, I wrote this while editing several fantasy novels, so I was in the mood. This has appeared a few places, but I've kept it to myself for more than a decade. It's here now—here as the book nears its conclusion—because it says something I think needs saying. Or something I want to say. Our bodies age, our faculties decline. Would that they can sustain each other just a little bit longer. Would that we could sustain each other.

Supposedly quite rare, I am, a Face-Changer, though whenever I used to ponder the conundrum of how to count those who can instantly change their appearance, an ability for obvious reasons generally best kept secret, I inevitably concluded there might well be many like me.

Or I might be the only one left.

Forty turns and a summer since my birth, I was living my life well, having recently settled in as an officer of the court of the most benevolent of keepers, my own Master Malcolm, a gentle soul whose felicity was bound in the contentment of his small but loyal clan. I thoroughly delighted in surreptitiously employing my distinctive talents to benefit the Master and our people, it being so easy for me to assume any visage of my choosing. Thus, might I better move inconspicuously about the countryside to seek advantage in trade, to gather important political information, and to keep potential conflicts *yon*, lest they come *hither*. The sole scion of a long line of Face-Changers, I have never managed to explain such a magical skill, a form of "wizardry" to some who have discovered my secret, a godly anointment to others. However one might characterize this blessing, I was especially grateful for how it facilitated the most challenging of missions my Master ever set for me, a quest to scour the high regions and bring back to our modest keep the very embodiment of a true legend.

"Aye," said Master Malcolm that fateful night, "our elderly are deserving of some relief from their pains, and there's only one soul who can give it. I bid you to find and bring us . . . The Age-Eater!"

I had heard of him, but never truly believed such a magical being could exist, just as I never believed the tales of occasional woodsmen who claimed to have shared a fire with the Star-Maker, a grizzled old soul who drinks fermented juices until he sneezes sparkles that float skyward and fill the night with ever more twinkling stars.

The Age-Eater usually appears as a child, so the stories tell, most often a boy who might be coaxed to spend some days and nights in a welcoming keep, graciously accepting hospitality while carefully determining if any of the elderly are deserving of his skills. What comes next, they say, by whatever magic he and only he commands, is known to be very difficult for this child, a hardship to his very soul, one borne of the purest love for others, an acceptance of service to those in need:

He makes them younger by eating some of the years off their age.

I know, it stretches the imagination to believe such an unlikely tale, but it seems equally unlikely, I dare say, to think I can even now tell you this story while assuming any appearance of my choosing, from the image of a pretty little Plyth-girl with round red eyes and curled blue nose, to a fat-jowled tessininker swine with his puss a mat of yellow downy fuzz.

The way the Age-Eater's feats are explained is that he consumes the years in a way that brings them upon himself, then departs to continue his travels, taking the weight of those years with him so that others might enjoy one last taste of the youth they had left so long behind. What he does with those years before he is able to appear again at another village or keep, his youth restored, is left to the realm of pure speculation, but surely, some say, there must a very harsh price he pays the gods for so fantastic a miracle.

"Just a legend, I dare guess," said the boy who graciously accepted me at his fire nearly five fortnights into my quest. He studied me with round emerald eyes, reflections of flame dancing in their depths, then ran fingers through his generous flow of yellow-brown hair before looking away. I would have guessed him to have passed no more than twelve or thirteen turns, tall and slender for his age.

"Is the very notion of a Face-Changer relegated to the realm of legends, as well?" I asked, having presented myself as a man of forty turns, a courtier weary from travel, a lone soul seeking company in lieu of building my own lonesome fire.

He looked at me again, his appraisal casually masked, a wariness expected of any child traveling without guard when the forests teem with dangerous beasts, the worst often walking on two legs. He smiled and looked away again. "Yes, another legend."

"Were it true," came the voice of a dark-skinned Kadoug woman whose face I suddenly wore, "ye boy would 'ardly see at what y'be seeing at right this very now!"

His head snapped around, those emerald eyes wide, the bottom row of his ivory whites showing because he'd dropped his jaw nearly to his lap. I tried to hold character, but the boy's reaction made me laugh, and by the time I again assumed my normal appearance of forty-turn courtier with alabaster skin, the tears flowed and my gut ached from spasms of hearty guffaws. The lad joined me in my mirth, proving I had won a new friend, my gamble at earning his trust paying handsomely.

"It is quite risky," he said, barely having regained his composure, "and therefore quite rare that one such as you would dare reveal his secret."

"But not," I countered, "in revealing it to one whose own secret is greater."

"Oh, were that so," he said, though a twinkle in his eye betrayed resignation to having been found out, except that he might still choose, even if only of habit, to parry a while longer.

"I have trailed you for more than fifty nights," I admitted, "and I was present in another form at your celebration in the stronghold of the Stockbridgin Clan."

"I suspected a false face," he said matter-of-factly, now lying back and propping himself on elbows, his nearly outgrown hose stretched tight, his green felt tunic freshly washed. "Followed often, I am," he admitted, "sometimes by those who mean to take that which I would not readily give, but I always succeed in evasion. How is it I failed with you?"

"Perhaps it is because my intentions are pure, the request I convey from my Master entirely beneficent. We are kindred souls, you and I, making use of our talents for the good of others, asking nothing substantial in return. How could the gods *not* want us to meet?"

"Perhaps," he said, not convinced. "Or maybe in my own old age I have simply grown careless." He tried to smile, but failed miserably in the attempt.

After toying with truth until we both grew weary of the game, my young friend agreed to join me on the morrow for a day's ride to my Master's keep, my steed non-plussed by the modest addition of a child's weight and his travel-pack strapped to an overlong walking stick. Of course, my people welcomed him as they would any traveler of benign intent, their only quarrels being over who might enjoy the privilege of hosting his next meal or providing him with a warm bed near a modest home's hearth.

He dwelled for a fortnight among us, the secret of his true nature carefully guarded, by which time he had come to know all of our people, even as he had taken special interest in spending time with the most elderly among us. He confided to me that leaving the embrace of so loving a community would prove, as it often had, to be the greatest burden borne of a mission to help others enjoy their remaining lifetimes.

His selections made, he asked me to accompany him as he visited the families of eight elders. There in the privacy of their homes, he revealed his true skills, offering his greatest gift: "You will plan a celebration for all to attend, a farewell party for my last night among you, during which I will invite each of the chosen elders to share with me a simple dance, even as your bones ache and your legs protest such unreasonable demands, and together we will achieve a moment of grace, an instant of pure joy during which I will consume ten years of your age and all the infirmities that came with them. Then as the hour grows late and the Star-Maker sneezes to fill the sky, I will be an old man who slips into the darkness. I will leave you a measure of restored youth as my gift, gratitude for your hospitality, a blessing to squander or cherish."

In every instance, the families wept with joy, the elder loved ones reaching out with tentative hands to embrace him, their fingers gnarled, skin like translucent parchment, eyes a-sparkle with hints of youthful anticipation.

Later my young friend and I sat before my own hearth's fire, enjoying hearty tankards of sharp cider. "How is it you chose certain elders, but not others?" I asked.

He gazed sadly into the flames. "I cannot help those who *want* to be old," he explained. "They have rushed eagerly into their dotage and demanded that it define their very existence. I cannot eat what is not graciously given, nor will I risk angering those unwilling to accept my gift. I seek those whose hearts strive to be young, even as their bodies betray them, and I know they will earn the currency of youth only if they surround themselves with friends and family eager to help them spend it."

I poured him more cider, even as I wondered whence comes such wisdom to a mere child. Surely the time he had spent suffering the pain of others' eaten years brought to him some measure of learning, a renewed appreciation for what he gives; but an even greater mystery vied for my attention: "Tell me, my friend, where does the age go when you have finished with it?"

He swirled his tankard and cast his gaze into its honeyed depths, then sighed as he considered his words. Finally, in the soft high pitch of a mere boy, he said, "You have proven yourself my only true friend in this world, which will make it even more difficult to move on, as I inevitably must."

I wanted to withdraw the question, to respect his secrets even as the purest act of friendship, to accept that I will never understand this talent that I coveted but would never possess, but he interrupted my thoughts as if to show that the fire of friendship is most assuredly kindled with trust.

"Lies always find words to live among, but truths sometimes dwell beyond that which can be said aloud. Truly, I fear that my every attempt to answer your question might diminish my very ability to serve others, so I pray you remember that my heart is pure, and when you find yourself traveling some country road or tarrying for a moment in the most unlikely of places, you will discover that I have passed that way. You will note simple changes only the sharpest eye might divine, a sapling grown surprisingly fast into majestic tree, wildflowers blooming early and strong even before winter wanes, baby schmeling kits grown surprisingly old and fat though they yet be yearlings, and maybe that rare night when the sun sets early so the Star-Maker can express his newfound youth by filling the sky with more sparkles than any man has ever witnessed."

He looked up and smiled, then stroked his whiskerless chin and wrinkled his nose mischievously, and for an instant I thought maybe I understood whence comes so great a power, but then I made the mistake of trying to analyze the construct of my rickety reasoning, finding myself left to smile blithely along with him, my notions for deciphering the universe fallen to shambles at my feet.

So Master Malcolm declared a night of starlit celebration in the keep's square. Roasted meats and hot breads and great steaming mounds of produce from the fields spilled lavishly across wide tables. The Music-Makers sang and played their pluck-plucks with glee. Every soul attended, young and old alike, dancing and laughing even as they tasted the joys of freedom and haven in a land of bounty looked after by our beloved Master. As the crowd grew giddy with delight, rumors of an Age-Eater whispered about, even as all knew that lo in this era of legends nothing matters more than sharing time with a departing friend.

Then as the party grew most raucous, the Age-Eater approached his selected elders one by one, reaching out to touch them, helping them to their feet and leading them to the center of the square. He would hold them tightly, then carefully sway with the music, helping them find their own tempos, the meter of their very souls, for each the rhythm of a lost youth. Some say they witnessed a nimbus swirling around the pair, and I think that maybe once or twice I witnessed it, too, but there is one thing of which I can always be sure:

It worked.

One by one, they grew younger.

Yes, their appearances changed, a few wrinkles smoothing, a hint of rosy glow returning, but youth also showed its glorious face in the depths of their eyes, in the way they danced and laughed and reached out to hold their own loved ones. People who had grown so weary of pain and stiff joints that they rarely, if ever, left their beds now kicked up their heels and shook their tail feathers like Kasee-birds delighting in an after-rain gorge of fat worms.

But I also watched my young friend grow old, aging a bit more after each dance, his face puffing for a time with the excess of middling age, his cheeks eventually growing sallow as deep lines traced the contours of a visage that has witnessed sorrows amid joys. His hair thinned to expose a mottled pate, an old body now stooped over and protesting every move with pain and stiff joints.

And for this I loved my friend.

I loved him for his sacrifice, his willingness to endure this burden at an age so soon before his own, for the pureness of his heart even as I finally understood that this task must inevitably bring with it a pervading fear wrought by the betrayal of one's own body. And though in that moment I discovered the undreamed of heights to which true friendship soars, it was I who most betrayed him that very night.

We slipped out undetected, leaving the celebrants to their enchantment, my heart breaking at the sight of him leaning on the overlong walking stick and struggling with every step; and all he asked of me was to ride him to some point several hours distant and leave him be, to turn away and not look back, to let him go with the cherished memories of what we shared leading to this most magical of nights.

I did do all that for him, but I failed in the most important part, for I could no more leave this gentle old man alone in the dangerous wilderness than I could leave him as the mere boy he would eventually become. I tried to ride away, but I turned back, walking the final distance, my stealth self-serving and deceitful even as I pretended I merely wanted to ensure his safety.

As I crept toward his fire, I heard the voice of that old man behind me, and it startled me with its frankness. "I expected that you would return."

"I am sorry," I said without turning, my gaze cast to the ground, "even as I am *not* sorry. You called me your one true friend, and this I know verily, so in that I will never rest if I cannot know I have offered my every measure to ensure your well-being."

He hesitated before speaking again, his voice quavering but true, his words this time from the mouth of a child. "I—I hoped you would come back."

And when I turned to look, there in the faint firelit glow against a backdrop of Star-Maker sky stood the boy I had first met, his emerald eyes glistening.

"But how—?" I knew the question, but my words died in a tangle of thoughts.

"You deserve the truth," he whispered, his eyes filling with tears. "There is no such thing as an Age-Eater."

I stepped closer, but he stood his ground, all remaining hints of deception between us drifting away on the fire's wisps of smoke. "I have trusted you, my friend," I said tenderly. "Will you now trust me?"

He nodded slowly, the tears spilling down his whiskerless cheeks. "I am an orphan of Audell," he said, referring to the harsh and cruel region beyond the hills. "I escaped the beatings and fled to wander the hills, always living by my wits until the night I met an old man, the Age-Eater of legend, whom I found suffering his last days at the mouth of a cave where he had taken refuge from the storms."

"But you said there is no such thing as an Age-Eater."

My young friend offered just a hint of smile, no doubt recalling a fateful instant of complicity. "He had intended to die with his secret, but then he recognized two things in me: that in the pureness of my heart I would delay my travels to offer comfort to a dying man I might just as easily rob . . ." Then! Suddenly behind a matching face came the voice of a dark-skinned Kadoug woman: "He saw in me, he did, the skills of a Face-Changer, the proof bein' ye would 'ardly see at what y'be seeing at now."

So of course we laughed heartily, and we laughed some more even as we had on our first night, at least until I managed to put my dropped jaw right.

"But how—?" I finally had to ask. "How do you eat their age?"

He sighed and led me to his fire, sitting close as friends do when they're watching the darkness to keep each other safe. "All I eat is the hospitality of wonderful families. I simply help them believe, and they make the years fall away on their own." He leaned closer and wrinkled his nose, mischief in his eyes. "Ah, but it is within themselves that they find their youth."

I laughed again, then reached out to clasp the shoulder of my young friend, just as I've clasped his shoulder a thousand times and more in all these many turns since.

You see, as a traveling pair of Age-Eaters, we have enjoyed our lot, meeting wonderful people, graciously accepting the bounty of their tables and the warmth of their fires, always leaving them happier for having known us, countless souls who found in themselves that which we all too easily lose. Alas, I am so old now that I no longer can pretend to eat more than a few years from one or two, my face as young as I want but my bones protesting every dance, yet I do go on, knowing in my heart that friendship is what has given me these many more turns than any man has a right.

And still I call him my *young* friend, though even he is showing lines in his true face.

But today is an especially good day, even though at the fire last night, as we talked of how long the legend of the Age-Eater had been passing from one generation to the next, we wondered if it might yet endure beyond our own times. For just moments ago, we spotted him, a lad of barely ten or so, a street waif offering his labors for bits of food, his pink brow topped by a shock of flaming red hair . . .

Until a caravan of dark-skinned Kadougans passed by and the most remarkable change came over the boy's face.

I think we have found a new friend, and I wonder if we will need to teach him how to dance.

Time and Space

I wrote this short fiction because I was teaching a story-writing class and couldn't find a good example of second-person future tense. The result is a chance to speak directly to you, the reader, about what's coming. Oddly for an author who favors hints of magical realism to make a point, this one is simply real. Sure, everybody's details are different, but you'll do this. Maybe you already have. Thanks to Scott Watson, whose gorgeous photo of an old tractor in Inkster, Michigan, prompted the final story in this collection. And thanks to you for spending time with my stories, for spreading the word, for posting those 5-star reviews. I would like to think this one is about acceptance, but that's a journey we take at our own pace.

*T*here will come a time when you need your space.

Used to be, you could spend all day tracing the contours of your little world, following the grain, crisscrossing the rows, digging in the soil, then climbing the highest tree to survey the realm. The day will come, though, when it's way too small, and you're way too big.

That drafty old clapboard house will shrink. The furrowed brow of cropfield will grow tiresome. That woman patching holes in her mosaic of vari-hued Mason jars will look away, saddened by talk of futures and plans and that time that comes. The man in the field on that old red tractor, the one who holds tight when you sit on his lap and steer, he will pause to watch you walk away, but he'll never really let go.

Yet, go you will.

You'll go after hugging that woman on the weather-worn plank porch, her jars waiting patiently. You'll go after waving good-bye to the man on the old red tractor, his brow furrowed like the land. You'll move to the next town, next county, cross-country, 'cross the waters. And the world will expand all around you, often too big, sometimes not nearly big enough. You'll live and you'll learn. You'll love and you'll lose.

And sometimes you'll forget what you still have. That's okay, you'll think, because in those moments when you find the time, you *will* remember, so you call, you plan, maybe next week, next month, next year. You'll know all is well, each season after the last, a woman filling her Mason jars, a man tractoring the sustenance she seals and preserves.

We don't have to touch a thing to know it's there.

And you won't have to touch a soul.

So time will pass and you'll chase success, even catch your share to seal and preserve, but there won't be enough, not nearly enough. Then at the worst possible time while you're shining in the light, those people you love will pass with the shadows, and you'll have to go back,

back across the water, the country, the county, the town. You'll be in a hurry to fashion lists: arrangements, finances, property, possessions, mementos . . . Who need I tell? you'll wonder. Who'll want what? What need I keep? So much to do, so little time.

You'll turn down that familiar road, eyes straight ahead, but then have to look, to pull to the side. The old red tractor squats forlornly in a patch of scratchy grass amid unplanted furrows, its motor silent, seat empty, the backdrop painting pale purple swatches of intermittent cloud, their passing shadows dark-patching the sunlit treeline.

And it'll break your heart that a machine can outlast a man.

Then you'll realize that tractor is yours now. You have no use for it, you'll think, not even this very thing, a mere object, the tool that helped pay to send you away.

You'll step closer, then kneel and scratch at the soil, clumps through your fingers reminding how the earth moves with life of its own, and you'll discover the most exquisite beauty in what you've always known but have yet to learn.

You'll move on, up to the house, then step inside and listen, see the shelves lined with that dependable mosaic of Mason jars; but you'll reel and have to sit, brought low by empty spaces, empty jars, expectations unmet. You'll sample the hint of a notion about maybe finishing the job, but there's no way and no time—no reason, really—and you'll remember you've come, not to fill jars, but to dispose of jars already full. You can't take them all, would never consume them, but you couldn't begin to bear the idea of letting her efforts, his harvest, come to waste. Still, time is running out.

People will fill the house. They'll laugh and they'll cry, and some will explain to you how they see it all, just see it their way and you'll be okay, we've all been down that road, all that's bad is really just part of the good.

And you'll try. Really, you'll try.

But you'll know what you've always known: Much that's good comes with a part that's bad.

More people will appear, many bringing food, some grown right here. A man will approach, a man you never liked. He'll remind you that space is valuable, time is money, the fields already plowed, seed in the bins, just give him the word and he'll make the time to work it, maybe split a few dollars, and least not let a season and space go to waste. That will sound okay at first, prudent, even savvy. You'll hear about others whose specialty is cleaning and selling houses, just write you a check, and that will sound good, too, even prudent and savvy, because you truly don't have the time, and you know that when all these people have gone, you'll feel the emptiness of your drafty old clapboard house.

You've got a plan now, you'll think, but in the swirl of darkness that night all that space will surround you. You'll sample the hint of a notion that you might simply let go, but you know that you cannot. You did not come here to dismantle this part of your world.

You've come to find a way to keep it whole.

There must be a young family out there who can love this land, who'll savor that medley of sustenance now sealed and preserved in that mosaic of Mason jars, who'll fill jars of their own and hold tight while the wonder of childhood in a big world steers that old red tractor and, hopefully, just maybe, someday proves that when a man passes with the shadows, his world passes to the next man, and the man after, because this is how we live, each of us in our time, all learning to embrace this one simple truth:

The next man will outlast the machine.

You *will* figure that out, and when you do, you'll decide there's no hurry, and you'll be right. A field needs to lie fallow every now and then. When you work it too hard, worry it too much, you must give it time to rest, to restore itself, recharge, a breather when no one expects you to give anything of yourself.

Come back in a month, sooner if you can. The Mason jars will keep a while longer. They live to buy us more time.

Next time you come you'll set aside more days, weeks even, a month, and do this your way. You'll pack up and cart home what you value, yet leave for others what you most cherish.

You won't be in a hurry. That's okay. It's okay that a tractor, there in a field across town, the county, the country, the water . . . it's okay that a tractor can wait.

It's okay that a tractor can sit there against a backdrop of pale purple swatches and break your heart.

It's okay for a tractor to be still while the shadows pass. It's okay because you've decided to do this right.

And you will, you *will* do this right.

But you'll need some space.

You just need some time.

About Stephen Geez

Stephen Geez grew up in the Detroit suburbs during the American-auto domination. He earned his undergraduate and master's degrees at the University of Michigan—Ann Arbor. He retired from scripting/producing television and composing/producing television music, then expanded his small literary management firm into indie-publisher and multi-media company Fresh Ink Group. Now he works from a deck overlooking the lake in north Alabama, helping other writers share their compelling narratives with the world. Find him at FreshInkGroup.com, StephenGeez.com, GeezWriter.com, and GeezandWeeks.com.

Fresh Ink Group

Independent Multi-media Publisher

Fresh Ink Group / Push Pull Press

☙

Hardcovers
Softcovers
All Ebook Platforms
Audiobooks
Worldwide Distribution

☙

Indie Author Services
Book Development, Editing, Proofing
Graphic/Cover Design
Video/Trailer Production
Website Creation
Social Media Management
Writing Contests
Writers' Blogs
Podcasts

☙

Authors
Editors
Artists
Experts
Professionals

☙

FreshInkGroup.com
info@FreshInkGroup.com
Twitter: @FreshInkGroup
Facebook.com/FreshInkGroup
LinkedIn: Fresh Ink Group

Fresh Ink Group

Geez Novels

www.ingramcontent.com/pod-product-compliance
Lightning Source LLC
Chambersburg PA
CBHW061211170626
46809CB00003B/1317